ZANE PINNER

Encore

The show must go on

For the fam. Our movie nights are the best x

Acknowledgement

A heartfelt thanks to my generous first readers; Saria Phillips, Nick Carlson, Janell Phillips, Saul Phillips, Emily Morgan, Brendan Colley and Colin Leonard. Your support and advice has been priceless. Many thanks also to Catherine Pettman and Evan Maloney for your support and encouragement of the original concept and treatment.

Prologue

January 1928

"Listen," said Mr. Mastricoli, pausing halfway up the wooden staircase. He pushed his hat back a little and Violet could see the sweat beading underneath its brim. "I don't know what your husband told you about this place, but it's better if you let *me* talk to them. You understand?"

I'll speak when I speak, old man. Anger simmered beneath Violet's skin, but she held her tongue for now. Samuel had told her nothing of this place and even less about the debt they apparently owed. If her husband hadn't left for Beaconsfield this morning, only an hour before Mastricoli came knocking, she would probably still be none the wiser.

Violet peered up into the hallway, at the candlelit red walls, at the polished oak beams, the ostentatious candelabra. Fury washed over her again.

A whorehouse. Damn you for a misbegotten fool, Samuel. She wondered how often he had been coming to this place instead of working on their new home in Beaconsfield. Her sweet, loving, hard-working husband was quick to laugh, eager to please and – apparently – helplessly randy.

"Do you understand?" Mr. Mastricoli insisted. "I'm risking

quite a lot in bringing you here, girl. The club has a reputation to uphold. As do I."

"I don't care about your stupid club," she muttered, almost too low to hear.

His lips pressed into a thin line and his hands squeezed into fists, as though he wanted to seize her shoulders but didn't quite dare. A droplet of sweat dripped down his temple.

"This stupid club *owns* your husband, girl. Which means they own *you*. Even Hell hath no fury like… if you can't even show *me* respect, then I'll need to reconsider my association with you."

"I apologise, Mr. Mastricoli. I will follow your lead." She ducked her head with a submission that belied her fury.

Nobody owns my family, you greasy coward. She would tell them herself soon enough.

He grimaced. "Then keep your eyes low. And your mouth *shut*. Come."

The opulent hallway was straight and long. Enormous oil paintings, darkly lavish and uneasy on the eye, hung in heavy gilded frames. A plush red carpet matched the colour of the walls. Two tall men waited at the far end, their huge shoulders packed into spotless grey suits, their eyes sharp above identical scarlet neckties.

Without breaking his stride Mr. Mastricoli removed his hat and nodded to the enormous men. One nodded back, his expression never changing, and they stepped aside. Violet kept her back straight and her eyes forward as she passed beneath their gazes.

There was another set of stairs leading up to a plain wooden door. At the bottom step, Mr. Mastricoli paused again, studying Violet. The old man licked his thumb and, without warning, reached out to clean her cheek with it.

"Get *off* me!" Violet shoved his hand away, disgusted. "I'm not one of your… *girls!"*

He shrugged nervously. The two giant men were watching them.

"Listen to me Violet, you mustn't…"

Violet pushed past him and stomped up the wooden stairs, shoving open the door.

A dozen unfamiliar faces turned Violet's way as she swept into the room. Her steps faltered.

The men – they were mostly men, older men – were dressed in fine black and charcoal suits. Their collars were white and crisp, their faces grey and nondescript. There were two women in the room, elegantly poised in expensive dresses with long glittering necklaces that draped almost to their knees.

They were gathered around low round tables, sitting in black armchairs or standing with drinks raised. The walls were dressed in rich red curtains that hung from floor to ceiling. At one end of the room, a bar was being tended by a short, dreadfully thin man who wore an ill-fitting red vest. At the other end was a wooden stage bracketed by three short steps on either side. On the front of the stage, a small key hung from a nail.

One of the women wore a tight cloche hat of woven gold sequins that glimmered in the dull light. She was smiling at Violet, a tight, approving smile, as she stood and approached with her hands spreading wide in welcome. A gold ring topped with a smooth black opal gleamed as she reached for Violet's hand.

"Ah. The builder's wife." Her eyes cut to Mr. Mastricoli, who had quietly slipped the door closed and was heading towards the bar, his work apparently done. "Violet, I believe?"

Violet frowned at the woman's hands, wrapped warmly around her own. "Do I know you, *madam*?"

The woman's eyes narrowed. "No, I don't believe you've had the pleasure." There was a titter from the shadows.

Violet pulled her hand away. "It's a pleasure I'd be most pleased to deny myself, if it's all the same to you."

There was another titter, but the woman's smile faltered a little. "You are educated."

Presumptuous sow. "Educated enough."

The woman laughed, a dry and calculated sound. "Educated and proud. The simple builder's housewife, not so simple after all." She tilted her head, waiting, openly appraising.

Violet tried not to scowl. *That cloche would be worth more than my entire wardrobe.* She resisted the urge to cross her arms in front of her body.

"My Aunts taught me to read," she muttered.

"Good. Education separates us from the beasts."

"Not all of us."

The woman stiffened. "Indeed," she said, her voice quieter. "And your husband, Samuel? Perhaps not as refined as yourself, might I suggest? Not quite as well-read? Perhaps more... of a beast?"

There was another dry chuckle from elsewhere in the room. All eyes were on them.

"My husband is a good man," Violet said, her chin raised. "And even good men can be led astray."

"Indeed," the woman said again, disinterested. She plucked a brandy balloon half-filled with amber fluid from the bartender's wooden tray, then leaned over and spoke in the gaunt servant's ear, too low for Violet to hear. Then she sipped the

4

fluid, smiling at her again. "A good man. A very good man, one of our favourites in fact."

There was nodding around the room. Violet glanced around nervously. Some of the men were smirking. The other woman chewed her bottom lip, her eyes shining with barely contained excitement. Only the bartender wasn't looking Violet's way.

"And it is always difficult when a very good man, when a very good *friend*, does a very bad thing."

Violet narrowed her eyes. "I had no idea my husband had such *distinguished* very good friends."

"Well, he *doesn't*, actually. Not anymore. Now... now he has creditors."

A small door opened behind the bar. A young woman emerged – a girl, really - dressed in a diaphanous blue robe that clung to her slim figure and left little to the imagination. The girl closed the door and walked slowly through the room, ignoring them. She drifted aimlessly over the plush red carpet, not meeting anyone's gaze.

Violet felt her spine stiffen and her head swim. *You knew it was a brothel. You knew it was other women, what else could it have been?* But she was a prospector's daughter and a woman of the world. She had seen the working girls at the tin mines in Derby and the brothels by the docks at Georgetown. She would *not* be manipulated by this harlot.

"My husband has the same weaknesses as any man. Especially when plied with fancy drink and fancy words. If he has unsettled accounts, then I..."

"He certainly did develop a taste for the... fancier things." The woman's grin was a leer now. "In fact, I believe he would be enjoying a taste of something rather fancy even as we speak."

Violet shivered. "What do you mean?"

"You see, builder's wife, your builder has apparently convinced one of my finest girls to abandon her trade and leave this fine establishment of ours."

"And why would he do that?"

This time it was more than a titter – one of the shadows actually laughed, low and mean.

The woman shook her head. "Oh Violet. You see... some men will do almost anything for love."

"What?" Violet's voice was a rasp. "Nonsense."

"I'm afraid not. After several... visits... he became quite taken with the girl. Decided to make an honest woman out of her, I believe. Sweet, really."

Eyes downcast, the girl drifted past them, her blue robe shimmering. The woman in the gold cloche surreptitiously cleared her throat and the girl stiffened, then turned towards the stage. Some of the men watched her approach it with blooming smiles.

"Not my husband. Not Samuel. He never did."

"Oh but he did."

"You're wrong. My husband is a good man. A married man. He would never... never..."

He would never do that to me. She couldn't say it. She felt like throwing up.

"A good man. A *good* man. A man of such... such... *girth.*"

There was more laughter.

The girl had climbed onto the stage, her sapphire-clad skin shifting in the dim light. Some of the other men were standing up now. Raising her arms to either side, she turned a slow practiced circle, her face raised to the roof, the planes of her shimmering figure reflecting the chandelier's glow. When she had finished, she simply stood and waited, her head down, her feet apart.

"I don't believe you. You're a liar and I don't believe any of this. " Violet's breathing was under control. Barely. *I need to get out of here.* "I would know if he was... he was... Samuel would tell me. He's a hopeless liar and he's no creeping coward."

"No. Samuel is a good man. He seems intent on doing well by her." The woman leaned forward, eyes gleaming. "I believe he mentioned a little cottage in Beaconsfield. A white cottage, with a plum tree in the front yard."

"What?" Violet's stomach churned.

"Yes, that's right. She's been bragging about her new claw-foot bathtub, the one that's right next to the fireplace... she's been going on about it quite a bit. Tedious, really."

That's my bathtub. I chose *that bathtub.* A tear spilled over her cheek, unnoticed.

"Oh Violet," the woman said, opening her arms, apparently offering to comfort her. Violet stepped back quickly, glaring at her, glaring around the room.

"I'm leaving. Whatever debt you think my husband owes you, you can take up with him. After I'm done with him."

The woman cleared her throat. "My dear, Samuel is in Beaconsfield, isn't he? Left this morning?"

Violet stared at her.

"He's not coming back, and why would he? He's watching that lovely young lady soak herself in her claw-foot tub right now, I don't doubt. He'll be polishing his drill, hammering away with his hammer, all those kinds of things."

One of the men had joined the girl on the stage and was peeling off his expensive jacket. Violet's breath caught as the man picked something up from the back of the stage - an iron chain with a manacle cuff. She looked away horrified as he closed the manacle around the girl's bruised, slender ankle.

At the other end of the room, the bartender was busy filling glasses with ice and sharp liquor.

"As to his unfortunate debt... I'm afraid he took something that I *owned*. Something that belonged *to me*."

"He rescued her." It felt like the floor was falling away from beneath her feet, but she was steady. *Sweet, foolish Samuel.* "He saved her from you."

The woman cocked her head, surprised, and when she laughed it was with genuine humour. "Rescued her? He *bought* her. He knew the price, knew it well, and paid it without complaint."

Violet tried to swallow again. "He paid it? Paid it how?"

The woman grinned. "My dearest, sweetest Violet."

1

A cinema has a heartbeat. Moviegoers pulse through its ventricles, flooding the building with life, nurturing it with dreams of romance, of magic and tragedy. In the minutes before a film begins the air becomes electric and the heart thuds. After the show, the beat is softer, like a murmur. The audience, their souls satisfied, drift back into the real world and muse upon what they've witnessed.

Robin, with the care and attention of any cardio thoracic specialist, polished the brass handrails leading up to Cinema Four. He topped up the popcorn oil and soaked the heads from the soda machines. He opened the wooden theatre doors and closed them again, opened them, closed them, controlling the flow like a uniformed valve. He dipped ice creams into melted chocolate, turned them in the air while they set, tried to avoid getting chocolate on his gloves.

Robin didn't like having dirty hands. Up until just a few years ago, he had spent his entire life on the family farm at Karoola, a drab and dismal corner of the murky Tasmanian scrub. Work on the farm was cold, dirty and monotonous. The nights were endless and remote, spent lying on the floor in front of the iron stove in a wash of TV glow. He would read paperback novels and dream of other times and places, wishing they were *his* times and places, leaving dusty fingerprints in the pages from his never-quite-clean hands.

Much to his parent's disappointment, Robin never took to farming. Instead he grew in the same shape as his Uncle David, a shape that didn't quite fit the stultifying walls of the aging farmhouse.

Uncle David had left the farm and bought the Majestic Cinema long before Robin was born. It was a canny investment for a young entrepreneur from the Tassie bush. As the only movie theatre in Launceston - the State and the Star had both closed their doors in the seventies - the Majestic had been unwaveringly successful for a long time.

For Robin, 'visiting Uncle David' meant going to the movies. It meant *Goonies* and *Superman* and *The Karate Kid* and free popcorn and so much soda that his piss would become fluorescent.

They had visited every month or so as Robin was growing up, but when he reached high school the trips in from the farm became more frequent and less formal. Gradually, his parents stopped joining him. By the time he reached Grade 10 Robin would catch the bus into the city after school most days, help his uncle out for an hour or two, and then catch the late bus back to Karoola. His father, reliable and reliably annoyed, would pick him up from the dark bus shelter in their rusted out Kingswood HQ.

When Robin finished high school, David had made him an offer. *Come and work at the cinema. Make a good salary, live here for free, no power or water bills, get some savings behind you while you're young.* Robin would learn to usher first, and then to run the Candy Bar, the Ticket Box and finally, the Projection Booth. One day, he would learn to deal with advance scheduling, distributors, release projections and financials. *The whole business, part and parcel. A steady career for as long as you want it.*

Eventually, he would run the place. Probably sooner rather than later too - Uncle David, owner and manager of the Majestic Cinema Four Complex, drove a silver Ford Mustang which lived in a double-garage at his palatial home in Blackstone Heights. No wife, no kids, no worries – just a sweet house, a sweet car and a slick wave of silver hair. Retirement wouldn't be too far away.

Robin hadn't hesitated to agree. He loved his Uncle and he loved the Majestic and here was an easy ticket off the farm. He would be living in the middle of Launceston, instead of forty-five minutes away. He would have his own place. A *cool* place. He knew how lucky he was.

Robin's father had been furious. His mother was more understanding, but stood behind her husband in all things. Like David, Robin was still welcome in the little farmhouse – and no doubt always would be – but his visits became less frequent and more formal as the palpable disappointment became more difficult to bear.

The work at the cinema was interesting, technical and varied, but more importantly it was definitely *not* ploughing or sowing or mulesing or weeding. There was even a vague kind of prestige to the job; people loved the movies, it was a night out, a date or a family outing, an excuse to catch up with friends. Some would come in their Sunday best, others in their comfiest duds, others in costumes and capes.

Robin sold tickets, choc tops and soft drinks. He wielded his usher's Maglite torch like a lightsabre that could hush voices and pinpoint empty seats. He wound the 35mm film reels onto massive wooden feeder plates and stacked them next to the projectors. He vacuumed around the bottom of the heavy red velvet curtains that framed each of the screens. He rolled up reams of posters and dropped them into a carton in the foyer so that the kids could help themselves. He poured raw corn kernels into the popcorn machine's stainless steel kettle and shook butter salt over them before they popped.

Sometimes Robin would lean against the wooden hand railing outside Cinema Four, at the top of the seven steps that split the upper mezzanine from the foyer. From there, he could see everything from the glass doors of the main entrance and the Ticket Box, all the way down to the Candy Bar, rest rooms and the control room.

Large square ottomans with spotless claret cushions were arranged through both the mezzanine and the foyer. The wooden double doors of each of the theatres – Cinemas One and Four on the mezzanine level, Cinemas Two and Three in the foyer – were polished hardwood, but their weight swung easily on well-lubricated hinges. Everything was clean, presentable and in its right place. He saw that it was good.

The magic of the movies.

2

Some smartass had drawn a moustache on Madonna.

Robin misted the megastar's face with cheap glass cleaner and scrubbed away. He put his elbow into it, but the thin line of sharpie ink wouldn't budge and he soon sat back defeated.

Evita's run was almost done – crowds that had been thin to start with had trickled to almost nothing - so the poster wouldn't be up for much longer anyway. The other posters, in four lightboxes to either side of this one, hadn't been marked.

The cinema foyer was cool and dim despite the sunshine streaming past the front entrance just out of Robin's reach. The row of glass double doors teased him with snapshots of a Launceston summer – groups of teenagers on their way to the Basin with beach towels slung over tanned shoulders, pairs of shopping mothers corralling their kids towards the mall with promises of ice cream from Fitzgeralds, delivery trucks from the TasMilk depot zooming past with drawling test match commentary blaring from their open windows, a slow-moving drunk in a filthy blue singlet wobbling back into the pub across the street.

It was warm out there, warm and bright and blue. Definitely not movie weather. Robin sighed as three girls roughly his own age – nineteen, pushing twenty – glided past the doors without even glancing in.

Kill me, he thought, glum. *Kill me now.*

Robin was sick of cleaning. He replaced the *Evita* poster with one for the new *Mission: Impossible* movie and the line of sharpie disappeared against the darkness of Tom Cruise's silhouette. *That'll do for now.*

Fifteen minutes later he propped the heavy wooden doors of Cinema Four open. A scant few moviegoers, mostly older folk, wandered back out to the light of day. Some smiled and nodded *thank you* as they passed and he recognised a few of the blinking faces. Regulars. The main entrance doors sounded their customary rattles as the punters left the Majestic Cinema Four Complex and disappeared back into the real world.

Robin watched them go, then pulled the doors closed and climbed the double staircase up to Cinema Four. With only a hundred and twenty seats it was the smallest theatre in the complex. The thoughtful audience had left him very little mess to clean up – a coffee cup in the third row and an empty Doritos bag near the back. He binned them both, then eased through an unobtrusive door in the very back corner of the theatre. The door was unlocked but camouflaged and like most of the fittings throughout the building, was painted a deep claret red to match the theatres.

The Elevator Room was about the size of a powder room but with the same carpeted walls as the theatres and a set of sliding stainless steel doors. If Robin stood in the centre of the room and stretched, his fingertips could *just* brush both of the walls at the same time. Aside from the shiny elevator doors and the matching call-button panel, every surface was covered in fire-resistant red carpeting – the floor, the walls and the ceiling.

He pushed the call button and watched the numbers blink, then took the elevator down a single floor, yawning and stretching his back through the gentle descent.

The Projection Booths were three long rooms on three different floors, all accessed via the echoing concrete stairwell that ascended from the Candy Bar storeroom. The elevator only went to the bottom booth, which was home to the projector systems for Cinemas Two and Three, a small workshop, an even smaller bathroom, and a long row of dusty old cupboards.

The top booth housed the projectors for Cinemas One and Four, a small writing desk stuffed with ancient paperwork, and a tidy little kitchenette.

The third floor, at the very top of the concrete stairwell, was home.

He had been living in the long, narrow one-room bedsit for almost three years now, so it had every right to look – and smell – like a teenage bachelor pad. Even though it was at the very top of the building above Launceston's busiest street, he thought of the room as the Bunker because it was insulated, quiet and secure. Safe.

The Bunker had a small living area with a TV and a stereo, a bunch of mismatched furniture and a rumpled queen-sized bed. The movie posters that covered every spare inch of wall had been here for decades longer than he had, but he liked them and had left them up.

Not that anybody would have known if Robin had taken them down; hardly anybody else had been up here since Uncle David had handed him the keys to the building and an usher's Maglite torch. The Bunker was a jumbled mess, but it was *his* jumbled mess.

His bed took up the far end of the room and he plonked himself down on it, feeling the stir of a deep-seated boredom in his bones.

Working in summer sucks the big one. I need a day off.

The next show would come out in 45 minutes, too soon for even a quick nap. Sighing, he picked up one of the coffee mugs from next to his bed and was about to head down to the top booth's kitchenette when he noticed the flashing sensor light.

Oh. Bloody hell.

Above the Bunker's door was a security sensor panel, a metal box with an array of lights that corresponded to the motion sensors nestled in every room of the cinema. There were a few sensor panels throughout the building too and one in each of the Projection Booths.

The lights for Cinema Two were flashing fitfully as the small audience fidgeted their way through the third act of *Titanic*. There would always be some small amount of movement in the theatre during a show so that wasn't unusual, but the other flashing light - above a label that read <u>Control Room</u> - certainly was.

The Control Room was home to the cinema's electrical switchboard and the air conditioning panel but not much else. The AC's all ran automatically, so there was rarely a reason for anybody to go in there. Plus, it was *always* locked. The only key to it was in Robin's pocket.

I must have left it unlocked. Robin sighed, annoyed at himself. He couldn't remember the last time he had been in there. It could have been unlocked for days. He hurried out of the Bunker, taking the concrete stairs all the way down to the Candy Bar storeroom rather than waiting for the elevator.

The Control Room door was slightly ajar but behind it was

darkness; whoever was in there obviously hadn't found the light switch on the far wall. *Kids making out. Or smoking. Or both. Time to be the bad guy.*

He couldn't give a shit if the kids were smoking weed or making babies in there, but Uncle David trusted him to look after the place and so he would. He filled his chest with his deepest voice, ready to eject some stroppy kids, noting the sharp tang of sulphur in the air. *Gotcha.*

Robin swept into the Control Room and the door snicked shut behind him.

"Hello?" The darkness was almost complete - the room was a concrete box and no light leaked in – but he could tell that it was empty. Whoever had been smoking in here had left while he was running downstairs. He reached for his torch but his breast pocket was empty; he left his Maglite in the Bunker. "Goddamn it."

"Hello?" It was a young woman's voice, barely a whisper.

"*Shit!*" Robin jumped, his heart thudding in the dark. He swiped at the concrete wall, searching for the light switch. "Sorry, I didn't realise… the lights are just here somewhere."

"Help me?" A hand slipped into his. Her fingers were cold, her voice frightened. "I need to get out."

"Just a tic." His other hand wiped the cold wall as he tried to catch his breath. "Let me find the…"

His fingers hit the switch and the overhead light came on. An odd feeling of embarrassed relief washed over him, but only for a moment.

He was holding an old man's hand, an old man in a stiff charcoal blazer who was sitting with his back against the cold cement wall. Dropping the hand with a yelp of disgust, Robin took it all in quickly; the slump, the closed eyes, the hand that felt like plastic.

"Oh shit… mate! *Mate!*" Robin knelt down next to the old bloke, shaking him gently. The man was clean and kempt, his grey suit spotless, his face neatly shaven. "*Mate!* Are you all right?"

He gave the shoulder a firmer shake and his stomach sank as old mate toppled over from his slump to lay awkwardly on his side.

Old mate's *body*. Old mate was dead.

Robin's breath caught in his chest. Ice spread down his back and made him shiver.

Dead. Dead and gone.

I need to get out.

Time slowed down as adrenaline rushed into Robin's brain – he saw the blue tinge of the man's lips, the stiff collar folded over his scarlet necktie, the spent matchstick on the floor, the blood drying on his fingers.

This last detail made Robin's breath catch and he looked again. The man's hands were covered in angry purple bruises. Black scales of drying blood circled his wizened fingers. Resting near one hand was a flash of white, a piece of paper half the size of a business card.

Not paper. A matchbook. It was one of the old-fashioned matchbooks, a piece of cardboard folded in two over a tight double row of wooden matches. Droplets of blood were drying across the cover, shockingly red against the white cardboard.

The sight of bright blood broke the spell and the adrenaline freezing Robin's brain finally flooded into his body. He ran, shouting for somebody, anybody, to call an ambulance.

3

"There's no need to close the cinema tonight." The inspector told Robin and David later. He looked at his watch, at the cinema's front entrance, at his watch again. Somehow he managed to keep the impatience out of his voice. Mostly. "The poor bloke had a heart attack, it could have happened anywhere. We've contacted the family. You can get back to business as usual."

David was nodding, sombre. "It was bound to happen one day I suppose. Some of the pensioners just about live here."

"And he would have just come out of the movie too, right?" The inspector's question was directed at Robin, who nodded. "So, probably a bit disorientated, went looking for the toilet, went through the wrong door into a dark room and bam. Just unfortunate. As I say, these things happen."

"There was blood on his hands." Robin muttered.

"You noticed the blood," the inspector nodded, eyeing Robin. Then he sighed. "When people have heart attacks, they panic just before it really hits. He's gone into a dark room, no lights, no fresh air. He's panicked and it's hit him, he's thrown his hands around and probably banged them up a bit..."

"I left the door unlocked. It was my fault he was in there."

The inspector frowned. "No son, it wasn't your fault. There's a 'no entry' sign on that door, clear as day. Just unlucky."

Just unlucky. Robin nodded again, eyes down. The inspector put a hand on his shoulder.

"I'm sorry you had to deal with this mate. Nobody's blaming you, not in the slightest." He looked at David. "I think this bloke might have earned a couple of days off, what do you reckon?"

David agreed. "Of course. Why don't you head out to the farm for a few days, Robin? Visit your parents, get some fresh air."

Robin was already shaking his head. "I'm okay. Thanks Uncle David but... I'm okay." *How did I leave that goddamned door unlocked?*

David put his arm around Robin's shoulders. He had to reach up to do it, but the teenager leaned into him gratefully. "Then at least take the weekend off. That's an order. Buckley can cover for you. Go and see your mates, go and get *drunk*, go and get laid. Just get out of here for a bit. It'll do you good."

The inspector agreed. "You need to blow off steam after something like this. Police, fireys, ambos, we all do it. Go easy on yourself, mate." He nodded at them and left.

David sighed as the glass doors swung closed behind him. "Decent enough bloke, I suppose. Must be a bastard of a job. Are you okay mate? You did everything right, you know."

Everything except locking the bloody door. Robin smiled, but his heart wasn't in it. David looked him up and down.

"Take a hundred bucks from the ticket box. Go and blow it. That's another order." He clapped Robin on the shoulder and sidestepped towards his office. "Go and get changed and get out here, Robin."

"Okay. Thanks Uncle Dave." Robin watched him go, then turned back to the front entrance. The bright sun had ducked behind the pub across the street, but it was still early.

He pulled the matchbook out of his pocket and turned it over in his hands, still unsure why he hadn't shown it to the inspector, unsure of why he had even picked it up.

The cover of the matchbook *wasn't* splashed with blood at all. The bright red patches were the background of a simple two tone art deco design; the white parts made a woman's oddly arched shoulders and the unmistakable slope of a pert breast.

A name was scored in a neat red script over the blank, feminine torso; *The Ruby Club*. Robin had never heard of it – if it was a bar it had probably been closed for decades - but he sure could use a drink.

He decided to take advantage of the night off. *Bottle shop, then the gorge.* Maybe Jimmy or Dan would be up at the Cataract Gorge, drinking beer on the grass next to the pool or jumping off rocks into the first basin. Either way, the inspector and David were both right; it was time to get out for a bit.

4

S ummer faded into autumn with an unruly breeze and the evenings took on a softer, colder hue. Now that the sun was lower in the sky, it passed just behind the buildings across the street, no longer shining directly through the row of double glass doors that made up the Majestic's main entrance.

Robin was selling tickets to the Saturday night late shows, covering for Natalie who had called in sick again this morning. *Another big Friday night for that girl.* He would help get the shows in, then head upstairs to the booth for the rest of the night. Maybe with a beer.

The foyer was already lively and would be thrumming soon enough, mostly with hyperactive teens and the hipster set. *Wild Things* had premiered three weekends earlier and showed no signs of slowing down – that particular Saturday night, it was probably still the hottest ticket in little ol' Launceston.

Buckley had the Candy Bar shift tonight, which would keep him happy. Jo and Hugh, two of the other part-time ushers, were out on the foyer floor ready to smile and rip tickets in half. Uncle David would babysit the Projection Booth until Robin closed up and cashed out the Ticket Box.

Robin didn't mind working the Ticket Box – at least there

was a chair. Out on the floor with the ushers you could be on your feet for hours at a time on a busy night like this.

The queue for tickets stretched back almost to the glass doors, which banged closed every few seconds with a rattling clack that Robin would know in his sleep. They were still coming to see *Titanic,* and *The Butcher Boy* was enjoying a surprising run too – but mostly it was couples and groups in their late teens or early twenties, all forking out their precious dough to see *Wild Things* and that kiss between Neve Campbell and Denise Richards that was the talk of the tabloids.

Most of the punters were bouncing on their toes by the time they got their turn at the ticket window. Robin couldn't help but smile as he greeted them, took their money, printed out their yellow tickets and sent them on their way.

But not everyone was cheerful. An older couple complained about the price of their tickets and then grumbled about the voucher for two free choc tops he gave them. A huge bloke, tall and heavy and dim, belched unconsciously into the ticket booth and bathed Robin in a fog of sour milk stink. A thin, offended-looking woman insisted that somebody was smoking in Cinema Four, but neither Jo nor Hugh could confirm it and she eventually stalked away, muttering.

A group of university students were laughing boisterously, making little effort to hide the booze in their pockets and purses. The loudest of them, a tall guy in an ill-fitting op-shop suit, kept grabbing at his giggling girlfriend. She didn't seem to mind too much.

He saw Hugh clock that group too. Technically they weren't supposed to let booze into the cinema, but they didn't hassle legal age drinkers unless there was a problem and there usually wasn't. Stopping them taking their drinks into the show would cause more drama than it was worth.

"Four for Titanic, please". A man in his fifties, straight from the Tamar Yacht club, pushed an American Express card under the glass. Robin nodded and took the card, tapped the computer screen to ring up the tickets and waited for the EFTPOS machine to churn.

The students calmed down a little, though the tall guy and his girlfriend were still laughing and kissing. One of the girls in their group, short, pretty and bottle-blonde, peered around as she emptied a flask-sized bottle of vodka in to one of the Majestic's large soda cups. She clearly thought she was being pretty ninja.

Robin smirked. *Not quite smooth enough, gorgeous.*

At that exact moment the girl looked up and met Robin's eyes across the foyer.

Guilty, she cringed and tried to whip the bottle away... but didn't stop pouring. The vodka splashed over her hands, feet and jacket and when she tried to dodge it even more liquid sloshed out of the soda cup. By the time she stopped moving, clear fizzy liquid was dripping from her in half a dozen places.

She winced up at Robin in red-handed dismay.

Robin managed not to laugh out loud. Grinning from ear to ear, he handed four tickets to yacht club and barely registered the man's reply.

The girl was blushing, wiping her hands on a serviette she had apparently pulled from thin air, embarrassed... but optimistic. She raised her Sprite cup and shook it, giving Robin a coy smile.

He shrugged, still grinning like an idiot. *Mi casa, su casa.*

She gave a little bounce, beaming, and took a sip.

"Oi! Hello? Still with us, sunshine?" A bloke's face pushed up to the glass. Yacht club.

"Sorry what?" Robin blinked at him.

"My bloody Amex mate, are you gonna give it back or what?" The bloke's face was turning red. Behind him, yacht club wife and yacht club friends watched with near identical startled expressions.

"Oh crap. Sorry mate." Robin passed the card back to him and glanced back at the girl, who was also grinning now. Robin shrugged again and she covered her hand with her mouth, laughing.

"Keep it in your bloody pants cobber," Yacht club said, strutting back to his crew with a hero's gait.

Robin glared at the man's back, embarrassed. A few people in the queue were craning their necks to look over.

I hope she didn't hear that. If she did, she gave no sign – her friends had started moving and she followed them towards the foyer and Cinema Three. *Wild Things.* Of course. Robin watched her go.

"Hello?" The next customers, a girl in a Metallica t-shirt and her pimpled boyfriend, were watching him.

Robin sighed and turned to the couple. "Sorry. Hi. What would you like to see tonight?"

5

David was impatient to get his book work done, so as soon as the last show was in Robin climbed up the cement stairs to the projection booth.

The booth was ticking over nicely and all of the movies were playing as they should. Each cinema had its own Super Simplex 35mm projector coupled with an enormous platter system and a small surround sound mixer. A scoped lens would push the bright, shifting light through the projectionists' thin horizontal window, where it would prism and fragment through the theatre air, drifting through dust and dreams before finally coalescing on the flat, white, welcoming screen.

Robin spent a few minutes looking through the little windows into Cinema Three, but he couldn't pick out the girl's blonde hair amongst the packed rows. So he got on with his rounds, checking the platters and spools for kinks in the film, checking the audio meters for overhead in the volume, checking the temperature in each of the theatres.

He saw with a wry smile that Cinema Three was warming up. *Two hundred and fifty horny teenagers in a dark room waiting for the pool scene.* It was a wonder the thermometer hadn't broken.

He scooted down to the Candy Bar, giving Buckley and Jo a wave – they were rounding out their shifts by making choc tops ready for tomorrow's morning shows. Robin went to the Control Room door, fishing out his keyring.

Robin paused then, key in hand; he'd been in the Control Room a couple of times since he'd found the poor old bloke's body, but it still gave him a chill. *Maybe I should ask Buckley to come and stand here while I...* he shook the thought away, embarrassed. *You're not a fucking child.* He unlocked the door and went in.

The overhead light flicked on reliably and the air conditioners were humming their usual hum. Dust bunnies scooted across the cement floor, but there were no cobwebs at all – the Control Room was a sealed box with neither crack nor draft in its straight walls or twelve-foot high ceiling.

The air conditioner's control panel was at the far end of the room next to the main power switchboard. Robin pushed the down arrows under the Cinema 3 label, bringing the temperature down to 22 degrees. The tone of the AC's humming slipped down a notch and Robin turned to leave.

The stain on the floor stopped him in his tracks. He hadn't been trying to *ignore* the spot where the man had slumped over, not exactly, but he hadn't wanted to examine it too closely either. So it probably wasn't surprising that he hadn't noticed the stain.

The blood stain. It wasn't huge, maybe the size of a fifty cent coin, but it was there.

Nobody cleaned up in here, he realised with a cold shiver. *The cops didn't, I didn't, and Buckley didn't.* The thought bothered him, but he wasn't sure why. Maybe it seemed a bit disrespectful, or morbid. Or just plain lazy. Either way, he would clean it up himself, right now. He didn't come in here often, but he could do without the reminder every single time he had to turn down the air conditioning.

He's panicked, flung his hands around and probably banged them up a bit... but what did he bang them up on? Robin can't recall anybody asking. There were no other stains he could see, not on the floor, not on the wall where the man had slumped, nowhere. *If he hit something, surely it would have left a mark.*

He stepped back, looking at the clean cement. Nothing. Nothing... *except...* He shook his head, blinked and looked again.

There *was* a stain on the wall. It was the same dark crimson colour, only larger, messier... and almost three metres above the ground.

Robin had to lean back to look up at it properly. *It can't be.* He shook his head. *How could that old bloke have possibly reached up there?* There were no ladders in the Control Room, not even a box or bucket to stand on.

Yet there it was, a smeared bloodstain just a foot below the high cement ceiling, a perfect match for the smaller one between Robin's feet.

I need to get out.

Abruptly the room was colder. Hairs stuck out on Robin's arms as he walked quickly towards the Control Room door. *I am not running, I am not a child, he didn't just float up there and...*

He pushed the door open, letting in the warm foyer light, and tried to ignore the sense of relief that washed through him as David walked over.

His uncle was grinning. "It's heating up in there already." He eased past Robin into the Control Room.

"Yeah," Robin muttered, clearing his throat, still holding on to the door.

"Bloody hell!" David's dismayed voice echoed out of the room.

He saw it too. Goosebumps prickled along Robin's arms and he held his breath as he stepped back into the Control Room. But David wasn't looking at the blood - he was tapping furiously at the air conditioner's controls.

"Cinema Three's set to 41 degrees! They'll fucking cook in there!"

"What?" Robin felt another sharp tingling, this time in his spine. "But I just..."

"I didn't even know it went that bloody high." David stopped pressing buttons when the panel read 19 degrees. Somewhere deep in the walls was a heavy clunk as the huge air conditioner abruptly changed gears and then settled, humming purposefully. David gave him a relieved, slightly hectic grin, and mimed wiping sweat off his brow.

"I'll call Sparky and get him to come and have a look tomor... mate are you all right?"

Robin opened his mouth but found he didn't have an answer.

David put a warm hand on his shoulder. "You look like you just saw a..." He stopped in sudden understanding. "Oh. Are you right?"

"Yeah."

David considered him with concern. "You don't need to go in there if it's... if it brings back bad memories. Just ask me, or Buckley or whoever. You don't need a degree to run the air conditioner." He grinned at his own joke, but Robin just shook his head.

"Its fine, it's just... look at this." Robin pointed to the dot of blood on the floor and David studied it with a bemused expression.

"It's blood from the old bloke's hand. Remember, the cop said that he must had hit them on something?"

"The inspector," corrected David. "Well, we can clean…"

"No but look," Robin interrupted, turning to the other wall. "How the fuck did he reach up there, David?"

David leaned back and looked at the stain high on the wall. He glanced at the small one on the floor again, then raised an eyebrow at Robin.

"It's the same blood," Robin said. "Look. It's identical."

David crunched on a couple of chips then held the bag out towards Robin, who shook his head. David shrugged. "It's not blood."

"What?"

"It's not blood. How could it be?"

"That's *exactly* where he was sitting," Robin pointed at the dot. "I *saw* the blood on his hands. That's where his hand was."

David was shaking his head. "The police would have cleaned it up."

"Why would they?"

"Robin, it's not blood. That stain's been there for years, both of them have been."

"You've noticed them before? Both of them?"

David chortled. "Well no, but… of course it's not blood. Those stains aren't eight weeks old, they're eight *years* old, probably *eighty* years old."

Robin frowned at him, then looked at the mark on the wall doubtfully.

David tittered again. "Robin. There's no bloody way old mate could have reached that. Michael Jordan couldn't reach up there."

"Reach what?" Buckley asked as he stepped into the Control Room. He and David both liked basketball and would discuss it at length given half the chance. "What are you looking at?"

"That mark on the wall up there, look," David pointed.

Buckley followed his gaze and scoffed, hands on his hips. "Jordan would reach that, piece of piss."

"You reckon?" David was incredulous.

"Easily. Ea-si-ly. The guy can grab a one dollar bill from the top of an NBA backboard, he could reach that without even trying." He nodded at the stain authoritatively.

"Maybe if he had a baseball bat in his hands," David grinned.

Buckley rolled his eyes, then rubbed his chin considering. "That mark would be what, eleven feet? Jordan would be laughing."

"What about an eighty year old man in the first stage of a heart attack?" Robin muttered.

"What?" Buckley looked confused.

David sighed impatiently. "Just get Maria on to it, she'll be in on Monday." Maria was the cinema's part-time cleaner, an efficient and quietly fussy woman who mostly kept to herself. "Look, I wanna get out of here so…"

"Oh yeah, the soda machine's leaking out the nozzle." Buckley told David, then turned to Robin. "And there's a chick up at the Ticket Box looking for you."

Hello?

Robin's belly flip-flopped. "What?"

"You heard me," Buckley grinned. David was smiling now too. "Better get up there, Romeo."

Robin left them grinning at each other, his head filling up with helium.

The girl with the vodka? It won't be her. It couldn't be her.

6

It *was* her. She smiled as Robin approached and he felt his face respond in kind.

"Hi."

"Helloooo," she drawled, smiling. "Am I allowed to talk to you while you're working?"

Robin grinned, shaking off the unease of a few moments earlier. *She's so damned cute.*

"It's okay. My uncle owns the place, so…"

"Oh," she tilted her head, mischievous. "So you can do whatever you want around here."

"Something like that."

"Yeah right," she teased. "Like what can you do?"

"I can let cute girls take their vodka in to the movies, for a start."

She grinned, radiant. "Yes you can! And yes you did." Coy again. "Thank you…?"

"Robin." He extended his hand and she took it. Her fingers were cool and sticky.

"Evelyn." She didn't let go of his hand straight away. "Thanks for letting me get drunk in your cinema, Robin."

He couldn't help but laugh. "You're more than welcome."

Evelyn squinted at him. "Is it really your Uncle's cinema,

young Robin? You don't need to impress me, you know."

"Well I think I do, actually. Are you impressed?"

"Is it true?"

"It is."

"Then I am. No wait!" She raised a waving finger. "I'm *not* impressed. You have to *prove* it."

"Prove it?"

"Prove it. Show me where the projectors are," she said. "If your Uncle owns this place then surely you're allowed up where the movies are put on, right?"

"You want to see the booths?"

"Yep. I've always wondered what goes on up there. One day, I wanna make my own movies, so this could be important for me. Like, professionally."

Robin shrugged and nodded. "What about your friends?"

"They're all busy fingering each other, they won't care. Can you let me peek up there? Just for a minute?" Her eyes were wide and hopeful.

"I can do better than that. Come on."

He led her over to the elevator doors, which were nestled in an alcove next to the Cinema Four entrance, out of sight from most of the foyer.

"This is how we get wheel chairs into all the cinemas," he explained as the doors closed behind them. "But it also goes up to the Projection Booth. Or the Lower Booth, anyway."

"You know so much," Evelyn breathed, teasing him again. "Tell me more about this wondrous elevator!"

He chuckled, acutely aware of her closeness, and was almost relieved when the elevator shuddered to a halt at the bottom booth. Almost.

"Here we are," he motioned for her to lead the way. "Where

the magic happens."

He expected another derisive giggle, but she didn't seem to hear him. She was sweeping into the projection booth, her head swivelling and her eyes wide.

"Oh wow… look at all this!" The workshop was cluttered with tools and exotic electronics, old snippets of 35mm film, stripped wires, cable ties, nuts and bolts segregated in cabinets resembling tiny apartment blocks, batteries hanging like dead soldiers in jungles of wire, light bulbs of every size and shape imaginable.

She ran her hands over an empty film spool, then gaped at the loaded platters nearby. "And the projectors… they're *huge*!"

She skipped over to the Cinema Three window and peered into the theatre. "I can see my friends! And watch the movie! *You* must watch them all the time!" She turned to him, eyes bright, breathless with excitement.

"Yeah, over and over. I love it."

"Of course! Who wouldn't?" She gave *Wild Things* a last glance. Matt Dillon was flexing his muscles. "Aren't there four cinemas though? There are only two projectors."

"The other projectors are on a different level. There's another floor above this one, and then a top floor where…" He stopped, self-conscious. *Who lives in a goddamned projection booth? She'll think I'm a bum.*

"Can I see?"

"If you want, but there's not much more to…"

"I want."

"Okay."

He led her to the top booth, where *Butcher's Boy* and *City of Angels* were playing into Cinemas One and Four.

Evelyn glanced through each of the horizontal windows.

"Ugh, Meg Ryan,"

"I know. I liked her in that Doors movie though."

"Oh that *was* her, wasn't it? Hmm," she wandered into the kitchenette. "There's a kitchen. Does somebody live up here?"

"Uh, yeah. I guess so."

She peered at him. "Do *you* live up here, young Robin?"

He swallowed and tried not to flush. "Yeah. There's another floor upstairs."

"No. *Way*." She gripped his arm. "You *have* to show me."

"Really?"

"Please!"

"Okay!" Robin laughed. "It's nothing special, just a little bedsit."

"In a *cinema*. Are you kidding me? I had no idea there was all this stuff up here!"

"Come on then."

He led her up the last set of stairs, praying that the Bunker didn't stink too much, trying to remember the last time he cleaned up.

"I call it the Bunker." He pushed the door open and motioned her inside. "It comes with the job, I guess."

"No. Fucking. Way." She looked around, shaking her head; the two old armchairs and the tatty Chesterfield couch, the mussed bed at the end of the room, the movie posters coating every square inch of wall and roof. "So many posters! Look at them all! It's amazing!"

Robin was laughing. "You like my digs?"

"This is the coolest flat I've ever seen. Not even joking. How long have you lived here?"

"A couple of years now. It's nice and quiet."

"I bet. And nobody would ever know you were here." She

was still gazing at the wall of posters. "So cool. Do you ever party up here?"

"Sometimes," Robin shrugged. "I have a few people over, nothing too crazy. My uncle's been good to me. I don't want to trash his place."

She nodded, turning to examine him again. He felt his back straighten as she bit her lip and moved closer to him.

"And have you brought many girls up here?"

"No. These guided tours are expensive, I hope you realise."

"Is that so?" She put her arms around his neck.

"Uh huh." He slipped his arms around her waist.

"I'd better get my money's worth then."

They kissed. Smiled at each other. Kissed again. Grinned at each other.

They made out for the next twenty minutes or so, grabbing and grinding, kissing and tickling. At one stage they fell onto Robin's musty bed, but when his hand brushed the button of her jeans she pulled it firmly away.

"I'm not that kind of girl," she teased, kissing him again. "Not on first dates, anyway."

"Even though I let you get drunk in my Uncle's cinema?"

"Especially because of that. You're clearly some kind of pervert." She kicked at him playfully.

"You better believe it," he growled, grabbing at her. They kissed again.

Not long afterwards, a bell rang in the distance, muted but distinct.

Robin sat up. "The movies are finishing. I need to close up."

"Yeah." Evelyn was smoothing out her blouse, her cheeks flushed, a smile curving her lips. "I guess I should find my friends."

Robin took a deep breath. *Here goes nothing.* "Will you come back some time? When I'm not working?"

She beamed. "Do you want me to?" He kissed her again.

They went back down to the bottom booth. She wrote her phone number on an old Pizza Pub menu. Then into the elevator, where they made out one more time before the doors opened in the mezzanine. A few people were already wandering around in the foyer and more were streaming out of the cinemas, blinking and dazed.

She made a fuss of fussing over his uniform. "*I, said the sparrow, with my bow and arrow...*" There was colour high in her cheeks as she gave him a final chaste peck. "See you soon, *Robin.*"

They looked into each other's eyes and he wanted to grab her again, but she bounced away into the crowd before he could. He shook his head, grinning. *Man, I haven't heard that rhyme since I was a kid.* He was still grinning.

A middle-aged woman was struggling to open the wooden doors to Cinema Four and Robin quickly stepped over to pull the door open and pin it into position. The woman smiled gratefully and led a short procession through the foyer out into the night air beyond.

Robin watched for Evelyn and her friends, but he didn't spot them and soon enough he had work to do.

She said she would come back.

And he hoped she would.

Later, he was locking up the front entrance when Jo sang out to him.

"Rob-in… I don't suppose you would change the Cinema One marquis for me? The step ladder's in the Candy Bar." Her uniform was unbuttoned at the neck, her tote bag slung over one shoulder. She waved the stack of marquis letters at him – solid black capital letters on credit card sized pieced of clear plastic.

"Should have eaten your veggies, Jo, then you wouldn't have these problems."

"Very. Funny."

"I'll fix it." He nodded to the marquis in question – *City of Angels*. "Did you come and see that?"

"I brought mum last week. It was quiet even then."

"Here he is! Romeo Robin!" Buckley's uniform was unbuttoned too and his sunglasses sat atop his head even though it was close to midnight. He climbed the foyer steps with a skip and a big grin. His sleeves were rolled up, his arms dusted with butter-salt. "How did you go mate?"

Robin smiled at him and shrugged as he changed the sign.

"Wa-*hey!* Roll over Romeo, here comes Robin!"

"Come on man."

Buckley cackled and kissed the air. Robin snorted. The marquis above Cinema One now read *Space Jam*.

"Wait, what happened?" Jo asked. Together the three of them walked back down the foyer steps and into Cinema Three.

"A customer picked him up tonight," Buckley grinned. He put on a cracked falsetto that was oddly muted in the carpeted walls of the theatre. *"Excuse me, do you know the guy who was selling tickets earlier? Because he's sooooo gorgeous and I just neeeeed to kiss him on the dick..."*

"Fuck off Buckley."

"Did she really?" Jo was grinning. "Did you talk to her?"

Robin nodded, trying not to grin himself. "We're gonna hang out, I think."

"Oh look at his face!" Jo snorted to Buckley. "That's really sweet, Robin. Is she nice?"

"Yeah... yeah."

Jo beamed at him. "Oh *good*. You spend way too much time here by yourself, I'm glad you'll have some company."

Buckley pushed open the exit that was nestled in the bottom corner of the theatre next to the screen. "She's cute too. Way cuter than he is."

"It's true," Robin nodded.

The bottom exit led into a short dark hallway, which in turn opened to the staff car park outside. Robin held the external door open for them.

"You be good, Romeo." Jo teased as she pulled on her jacket. "See you next week!"

"Night Jo, see you then."

"Oh there's an open packet of Maltesers in the Candy Bar," Buckley called out as he unlocked his Datsun 180. "Don't you let 'em go to waste, Romeo."

"Just go home already."

Buckley cackled again.

Robin watched their cars light up – Buckley's boxy hipster-mobile, Jo's sensible little Astra – and pull out of the staff carpark. Their engines trailed away into the quiet Launceston night and Robin had the city to himself.

He pulled the self-locking exit door closed and walked back into Cinema Three. The creak of the door closing was muffled by the theatre's carpeted walls. Only the dim houselights were on and the big theatre was vast and shadowed.

Robin was buoyant. *Roll over Romeo!* He stopped in the middle of the aisle, taking a deep, satisfied breath. Excitement glowed in his chest. He could still feel the soft press of Evelyn's lips. The curve of her hip, snug in his palm. Her easy laugh, the way she had whispered into his electrified ear.

The empty theatre watched him saunter a John Travolta groove back up the aisle, his hips waving from side to side, his feet gliding across the carpet, one hand shaking jazz fingers, the other pointing rhythmically like a rock star at the empty rows of seats...

Somebody was sitting near the back corner of the theatre, watching him.

"Oh *shit!*" Robin gasped, stumbling over his own feet. He could hardly make the shape out amongst the shadows. He pulled the Maglite from his breast pocket and clicked it on. White light streamed from his fist.

It was a woman – he *thought* it was a woman, but the figure covered its face with gloved hands, hiding from the light. The top of its head was wrapped in a thin black rag that was streaked with gold thread.

"*Jesus*, you scared me!"

40

She didn't respond, but as he got closer he could see her shoulders shaking.

Is she crying? "Um. Sorry," he said, still shaken, stopping at the end of her row. "Are you okay? The place is actually closed… can I… can I…"

"Start the show."

Her voice was terrible, a gritty, choking rasp that made Robin's blood run cold. His bladder was abruptly unbearably full.

"No," he felt himself whisper. He shuddered, and the torchlight wandered.

The woman uncovered her eyes. The woman had no eyes.

Her face was a blackened ruin, burned and twisted into a charred, featureless mess. Still, somehow, he felt her furious gaze, her malicious glare.

"Start the show." The words grated like ashes on stone.

Gasping for breath that wouldn't come, Robin stumbled back. His feet tangled again, his knees bashing into an armrest and spilling him backwards into one of the cinema seats. He scrambled to sit up, thrusting the torch in her direction.

Nobody was there. The seat was empty. He pulled himself out of the chair and crept to the end of her row on shaking legs, peering into the torchlight. Nothing. A cold shiver flushed down his spine. The cavernous theatre was dead silent apart from the sound of his own throat trying to constrict. The torchlight shook as he made himself exhale. The theatre was empty.

You imagined it. Dust tickled his nostrils. Dust and ashes. Another cold shiver flushed down his spine. *Start the show.*

Something moved behind him, under the seats near the middle of the empty theatre. A heavy, dry rustle, like something was crawling along the heavy carpet.

No longer dancing, Robin scooted up the aisle to the back of the theatre. *I'm not running, I'm NOT running...* but by the time he reached the wooden double doors, he was.

He burst into the warm light of the foyer, letting it wash over him as he sucked in a deep, unsteady breath. *I imagined it. There was nobody there.*

But there *had* been. She *had* been, burnt and cold and furious. *You're seeing things, dickhead.*

The foyer felt very quiet. There was no traffic humming past the front entrance and even the lights at the pub across the street were out.

"Fuck this." Robin ducked through the Candy Bar and jogged up the cement stairwell, trying to ignore the echo of his footsteps, flinging open the Bunker door and shoving it shut behind him. *I'm done. If I've locked somebody in, they can bloody well sleep here for the night.*

He looked up at the sensor panel above the door. All of the lights were dark; nothing was moving anywhere in the building. *Seeing things.*

A small white cupboard near the Chesterfield boasted a range of glass bottles, all containing some amount of white or brown liquid. Selecting an almost full bottle of Southern Comfort, Robin drank a mouthful. When the burning in his gullet subsided he drank again. He sat the bottle on the coffee table and, with a heavy sigh, flopped into one of the Bunker's patchy arm chairs.

His TV was an old Sony Technicolour, solid and reliable, and switching it on was like waking up an old friend. He put on *Rage*, which would play music videos non-stop all night. The music chased away the quiet and the videos of grunge bands moping around Seattle and California made him feel less alone and it was easier to forget that, right now, he might be the only person around for a couple of miles.

He thought of those Maltesers, all the way down in the Candy Bar, but settled for another finger of booze instead. It wasn't long before he dozed off with the uncapped Southern balanced on the edge of the table.

And not long after that, the motion sensor in Cinema Three flicked on. It remained on, unblinking, until the deepest hour of the morning.

8

A shriek. Shrieking, painfully loud. Shrieking, searing into his sleeping ears.

Robin jerked awake, bleary and stiff. He was still wearing his uniform and the world tasted like a shoe. *What time is it?* He looked at the small skylight at the far end of the room and groaned. *Shit, it's late.*

The phone rang again, its analogue wail cutting through the quiet Bunker. He flailed over to it through a tangle of doona, snatched the handset off the cradle and flopped back down on the bed.

"Yep?"

"We gonna have some movies today boss?"

"Buckley. What time is it?

"Ten past Eleven."

Not too bad then. The first show on Sunday was always at 11.30am. "Have you opened up?"

"Not yet. Candy Bar's ready to go, we just need the floats. "

"Right. Thanks man. Give me five."

"You've got two."

"I'll take 'em."

He hung up, yawned, stretched, and looked around the bunker for a drink. *No bloody water. I must have passed out.*

His neck was stiff, his ass was numb and his shirt a crinkled mess... but he was already dressed for work, at least.

By the time he unlocked David's office, breached the old iron safe and delivered the cash floats to Buckley in the Candy Bar and Natalie in the Ticket Box, there was a small crowd gathered around the foyer entrance. *A bit of anticipation never hurt*, Robin thought. He wasn't sure the tired looking Dad with the four kids bouncing off him would agree.

The scent of stale popcorn, reheated from the night before, permeated the foyer. Robin pushed the glass doors of the front entrance open, smiling at the punters as they rolled in, then immediately propped open the wooden doors to Cinema One. *Space Jam* would kick off the day's entertainment in just a few minutes. *No sweat.*

He was about to dash up the stairs into Cinema One when Natalie called out from the ticket box, where there was already an impatient queue.

"Robin? Is that right?" She was pointing at the Cinema One marquis.

"Yep. It'll start a couple of minutes late," he called. "But the doors are open..."

"It's still *Space Jam* in there though, right?" Natalie nodded towards the Cinema One doors, confused.

Robin turned to go back up to the booth. "Yeah of course, I've just loaded it up ready to..." He stopped.

The marquis above the Cinema One doors didn't say *Space Jam*, or even *City of Angels*.

I Came Back For You.

Robin stared at it, confused.

That's not what I put up there. Is it? A cold shiver stroked his spine. Nobody else could have changed it. He glanced at the other marquis and this time the cold flushed through his entire body.

They were all wrong. Cinema Two's sign read *She's A Liar* whilst Cinema Three's was a single word, a question; *Sugarplum?* Cinema Four's marquis was blank.

What the hell was I thinking? It didn't make sense. He reached up and snatched the letters down from the Cinema One sign one by one. His hands shook. *How could I have...?*

"Excuse me," said a small voice at his elbow.

Robin jumped as if pinched, then blinked at the tiny elderly woman who had spoken. She was standing too close to him, was looking him up and down with watery, red-rimmed eyes.

"Huh." Robin tried to speak but nothing came out. He had no breath.

I Came Back For You.

"Could you tell me if we're allowed to take sandwiches into the cinema?" She eyed him suspiciously. "I've made sandwiches for us all, because the popcorn here is too expensive, and everything else here has too much sugar, they don't need it, and I told their mother when I picked them up this morning that I wouldn't be giving them any rubbish even if I had to..."

The paralysis was wearing off. Two slightly mortified high school girls waited patiently at the woman's back. All three of them were the same height and their faces were variations of a single sour theme.

"*You can...*" Robin's voice came out as a rasp, so he swallowed and started again. "You can take in sandwiches, as long as they're not toasted."

The woman eyed him as if he were mad. "Well they're not toasted, they're *sandwiches*. I don't carry a toaster with me." She rolled her eyes. The girls – her granddaughters, presumably – rolled their eyes as well with identical expressions of exasperation.

Robin excused himself and went back into the staffroom. The letters from *City of Angel* were still in a pile on the table. He got out the wooden box specially built to hold the letters and was looking for a **J** when Buckley came into the office.

"What's with the signs?"

Robin shrugged. "I put up the wrong titles."

"On all of them?"

Robin laughed, but it felt hollow. "Yeah. Must have been on autopilot."

"I'll say. Do you want me to fix them while you start the ad roll?"

"Thanks dude. I'm all over the place this morning."

"Geez I wonder why," Buckley chortled. "She coming in today?"

"I don't know. I hope so. Listen, can you give me a hand with something else once the shows are in?"

"For sure, just sing out."

"Cool, I will do."

Robin left him to sort out the marquis and went back up to the booth. *Space Jam's* ad reel kicked off a few minutes later. He went through the routine, firing up the other three projectors and their sound systems, loading up the ad reels, setting the stage curtains, starting the shows. All four movies started on time. The building quietened as the double-doors of each theatre eased shut.

Robin marched purposefully downstairs to the cleaner's cupboard in the men's toilets. From there he retrieved a mop and bucket, a bundle of rags and a spray bottle half-filled with an unnatural pink liquid. When he came out of the gents,

Buckley was standing in the middle of the foyer, his face slack with dismay.

"Cleaning?" Buckley backed away, horrified.

"I'll clean," Robin said quickly. "Can you just grab the ladder? And then maybe spot me?"

"The big ladder?"

"Yeah. Thanks. It's in the bottom booth."

While Buckley went to fetch the ladder, Robin half-filled the bucket with hot water in the Candy Bar's sink then lugged it back out into the foyer. He unlocked the Control Room door and propped it open, setting the bucket down on the cement floor next to the blood stain.

Right. You're gone. When Buckley arrived with the ladder a couple of minutes later, Robin was already scrubbing away. The little stain was fading.

"Thanks, just lean it against the wall," Robin told him.

"No worries." Buckley sat the ladder down then bent over and scooped something off the floor. "Ooh ah, check this out.

"What?"

Buckley held out a spent matchstick, the top half of it blackened and burned. "Bloody smokers, eh? Sneaky little pricks. What *is* that stuff?"

Robin sighed and sat back on his haunches, warm water running pink around his knuckles. "I think its blood." Buckley looked blank. "Old mate's blood. The old fella that died in here, remember?"

"I thought he had a stroke."

"A heart attack." Robin thought of the cop's words. *He went through the wrong door into a dark room and bam... just unlucky.* "And he banged his hands up a bit too."

"And that's his blood."

"Yeah. And…" He gazed up at the larger stain, high on the wall.

"Oh right," Buckley scoffed. "That's not blood. How the fuck would he get it up there?"

"I don't know."

"Jordan could do it. But not old mate, I mean…"

"I know. I know. But… it's his blood. I'm sure of it."

"So you're gonna clean it up? Maria's in tomorrow."

"It's creeping me the fuck out." Robin shrugged, annoyed. He sprayed the pink cleaner into the air, a warning shot. "Can you hold the ladder?"

Buckley held the ladder. Robin climbed up, the pink spray and a couple of wet rags in hand. He tackled the stain with grim determination, spray, scrub, spray, scrub. It was stubborn at first, but once it started lifting the rest came away easily enough. A few minutes later and it was just a memory.

"Thanks," Robin told Buckley as he descended. He felt better. Lighter.

They packed the ladder and cleaning gear away with about half an hour to spare before the first show came out.

Robin yawned. "Is everything else okay? I need a shower before the next shows go in."

"Yep, go for it." Buckley seemed preoccupied, so Robin left him to it.

9

After a hot shower, a hotter coffee and a slice of third day pizza, Robin was ready to function properly. The afternoon was bright and still and clear. Patrons came in wearing t-shirts and light blouses despite winter being only weeks away.

And then, just before 3pm, the patron he had been hoping to see the most came in.

Evelyn smiled brightly when she saw him leaning against the Candy Bar counter. She skipped down the foyer steps but hesitated at the last. Robin opened his arms wide in greeting and she flew into him. He squeezed her and she squeezed him back and he was glad.

"Hi." Robin knew he was grinning like a fool, but he didn't care.

She was smiling too. "Hello young Robin. Is this a bad time?"

He waved a hand at the expanse of empty foyers. "You've managed to fight your way through the crowd, so I guess I can make time."

"You're funny."

"What are you up to?

"Well, I'm talking to you, clearly." She poked her tongue out. "I had to pick up a book from Birchalls, so thought I would drop in. Do you finish work soon?"

He shook his head. "Not until close."

"Aren't you the boss? Tell them you're taking the night off."

"My uncle's the boss and he's already taking the night off."

"Well then quit," she pouted. "No don't quit. Your job is awesome."

He laughed. "Maybe we could hang out tonight? Here, I mean. We could watch a movie." It sounded worse than lame, but before he could snatch the invitation back she nodded, blushing a little.

"I'd love that."

Relief flooded through him. "Me too."

Neither of them spoke for a moment.

There was a cough from the Candy Bar storeroom, loud and deliberate. A moment later Natalie appeared, pushing the choc top cart to its customary position behind the Candy Bar.

"Hi!" She waved at them. "Ignore me! I'm just setting up the choc tops." She ducked down behind the cart, fussing with rubber gloves and waffle cones - but Robin could see her peeking at them over the tub of melting chocolate.

He rolled his eyes theatrically. Evelyn giggled and walked over to the Candy Bar.

"Are you making ice creams?" She asked.

"Choc tops," Natalie corrected. She demonstrated. "Scoop the ice cream into the cone… dip it in the chocolate… and let it set." Her choc top was cue-ball round and evenly coated, not a drip to be seen.

"Mine never look that good," Robin confided to Evelyn.

"Is that full of melted chocolate?" She was looking at the bubbling pot in the centre of the station. "It looks amazing!"

"The smell gets to you after a while," Natalie said. She

squinted at Evelyn. "Hey I know you. You went to Queechy High, didn't you?"

Evelyn was nodding. "I was in your sister's grade."

"That's right!"

"How is Amanda?

"Still in San Francisco, having the time of her life." Natalie shook her head. "You were in the big play they put on that year, weren't you! Eve?"

"Evelyn."

Natalie giggled. "That's right, sorry. You were *so* good in it, I loved the song you and the guy did... *Down on skid row*?"

"Oh wow, you remember." Evelyn was blushing.

"I had goose bumps!"

"You're a singer?" Robin asked, impressed.

"She's an *actress*," Natalie told him. "A really good one too."

"Stop it," Evelyn flapped a hand at her. "It was just a school play."

"But you're still doing acting, right?" Natalie demanded. "You definitely should be."

Evelyn hesitated, then nodded. "I'm going to NIDA next year."

Natalie gasped. "You're *kidding*? Oh my *god c*ongratulations!"

"That's amazing," Robin added, a bit stunned. *Holy shit. She must be good.*

Natalie glanced at Robin and her excitement ebbed a little. "But NIDA's in Sydney, isn't it?"

Evelyn nodded. "Yeah. My parents are looking for a flat there now." Her eyes flicked to Robin too. "I'll move up there in September. Well. That's the plan anyway." She shrugged.

Natalie shared a sympathetic glance with Robin but couldn't help but grin at Evelyn. "I'm so happy for you Evelyn, congratulations. Amanda will be over the moon!"

"Tell her I said hi?"

"Of course!"

They waved, still beaming at each other, and Robin lead Evelyn back up to the Ticket Box.

"What was the play?" Robin asked her as they approached the entrance way.

"*Little Shop of Horrors.*"

"You were the lead role?"

"I guess. My dad had a tape of the movie, so I just learned all the songs before the auditions."

"Gorgeous *and* modest," Robin mused.

"And leaving before I get any more embarrassed," she finished. "What time should I come back?"

"The last shows are in by 9pm. Any time after that?"

She pecked him on the cheek, sweetly chaste. "I'll see you then, young Robin."

He watched her walk away, his stomach flipping around in useless circles. *I'll see you then, young Robin.*

Shaking his head, wondering at his luck, he walked back downstairs in a daze.

"Wow Robin, nice catch!" Natalie called out to him. She was elbow-deep in one of the huge cylindrical ice cream buckets - boysenberry.

He shimmied his shoulders a little. "And you know her!"

"A little bit. She was really good in that play."

"I believe it."

"And she's super pretty too."

Robin shrugged, but couldn't help his grin. "We only just met, but... we hit it off, I think."

"Obviously. You like her?"

"Yeah. She's fun."

"It's about time you had a girlfriend, Robin."

"Maybe… but she's leaving, right?"

"In six months."

"Yeah."

Natalie snorted "You're gonna go for it anyway, right?"

"Abso-*fucking*-lutely."

Natalie bounced on her toes as she went in for another smooth scoop of boysenberry ice cream. "Oooohhhhhh! Robin's got a girlfriend, Robin's got a… oh!" She frowned.

"What?" Robin knew he was blushing, but Natalie wasn't looking at him anyway. She was frowning into the ice cream bucket, pushing with the scoop. Robin heard a soft *tink*.

"There's something in here… look." She pulls the scoop out and lifts it gingerly. Frozen in the berry-streaked vanilla ice cream is something small, grey and hard-looking. "Is that a marble?"

She gently probed the ice cream away with a gloved finger… then gasped. With a horrified cry she dropped the scoop, ice cream and all, and it clattered loudly on the tiled floor.

"*Nat?* Are you all right?"

She looked ill. "Oh my *god* Robin."

"What is it?" He peered over the counter. The scoop had bounced, streaking a creamy trail across the tiles, and now he could see the grey thing protruding from a melting glob of boysenberry.

"It's a tooth." Her face was white, almost green. "It's a fucking *tooth.*"

She was right. He could see the pearly grey tooth, its dark roots slowly emerging from the melting ice cream. *It's big*, Robin thought, his mind reeling. *It's a big tooth.*

"I'm going to be sick." Natalie retreated back into the storeroom, peeling her gloves off and throwing them onto the candy bar floor.

"That's rank," Robin wondered, his voice thin. "Are you okay, Nat?"

But she was heading for the ladies, shaking her head. When the door closed behind her, Robin leaned on the counter again, staring. The ice cream was melting around the tooth and it seemed to be growing longer. *Blood, now teeth. My lucky day.*

I Came Back For You.

He took a deep breath and went to get a bucket.

10

The late shows were quiet. *Titanic* started an hour before the others, so was in and out of the way nice and early. *Wild Things* had a smaller, older crowd tonight – it was a school night, after all – and *Butcher's Boy* had less than a dozen punters.

Although she was laughing about her grim discovery now, Natalie refused to go anywhere near the Candy Bar and Robin let her leave early. They had found four teeth, all told. Buckley carefully scooped through the rest of the boysenberry until he was sure there were no others hidden amongst the swirls. Robin went through the freezer and found a few other buckets with the same or similar use-by dates, pulling them out to go back to the supplier. Buckley wanted to check them for more teeth, but Robin shooed him away.

Buckley, sulking, fished out a new promotional stand from the staffroom and unpacked it all in the mezzanine. Promo stands could be as simple as a cardboard cut-out with a flat base – if you were lucky. More and more often they were enormous, complicated, laminated jigsaw puzzles. Some were three dimensional interpretations of the movie's title sequence, some had posing actors or menacing monsters looming up to the ceiling, some even had moving parts or lights or sounds. Those ones always seem to require some proficiency in engineering.

Buckley, not an engineer, could spend hours putting one of the more complicated stands together. He usually got there in the end. Usually.

Robin helped pull some of the huge cardboard panels out of their boxes and lay them flat on the floor. The instructions, written in scattered English with little correspondence to reality, were more or less useless except for the fact they showed a drawing of the finished stand.

"*The Truman Show*," Robin read.

"Yep," Buckley held up three tiny light bulbs and their cheap looking plastic sockets. "So a frame with the poster on the front and these lights go behind it?"

"I think so."

As Buckley untangled the wire that connected the sockets to the enormous power adapter, Robin started lining up the slots on the long, thick slices of cardboard. Customers glanced over on their way to the Candy Bar or the toilets and one woman in a pale yellow blouse even laughed at them cheerfully.

"Looks like fun boys," she grinned, striding with the unmistakable tension of somebody busting for a piss.

"The magic of the movies," Robin sighed and she laughed, hurrying down to the ladies.

They folded, clipped, swore, bent, slotted, ripped, gave up, restarted, wired, plugged... and eventually stood back and admired their work. Buckley flicked the power switch on and off a couple of times; the difference was negligible. The strategically placed bulbs, which had taken twenty minutes to wire in properly, did nothing. The overall effect was underwhelming; it was a big box with a poster on it.

"Shit," said Buckley. He was right.

"The Truman Show."

Robin's stomach flipped at the sound of Evelyn's voice. She was standing just behind them, assessing the stand with a doubtful expression. The wind had caught her hair and her cheeks were bright from the cool night air.

"It starts next month." He kissed one of those lovely cheeks. "Hello."

"Hi," she smiled. "Am I too early?"

"Nope. Perfect timing."

"We just finished this origami masterpiece," Buckley gesticulated proudly. "Does it make you want to see the movie?"

"Um. It sure is a big poster," said Evelyn.

Buckley threw up his hands and marched away in disgust.

Evelyn blinked. "What did I say?"

Robin laughed. "Don't mind Buckley, he's a drama queen." He considered. "Like you, I guess. Queen of Speech and Drama."

She punched him in the arm. "I loved Speech and Drama."

"I bet you did."

"And you were, what, carving a pair of salad tongs in Woodwork 101?"

"My high school didn't have a drama department. I don't think they did, anyway."

She looked at him in disbelief as he led her down to the Candy Bar. "You don't know whether your high school had a drama department? Which high school did you go to?"

"Ravenswood."

"Ravenswood. Is that the one that burned down?"

"That's the one. The fire was halfway through grade ten. They shut the school down and told us all to go to Brooks to finish the year." He shrugged. "I didn't bother."

"You never finished grade 10? Or went to college?"

Robin shook his head. "There wasn't much point. My Uncle offered me a job here and the Bunker to live in…"

"And someday you'll be the boss."

"I guess so. David doesn't have any kids, and he wants to retire in the next few years…" he shrugged. "If I don't fuck it up, I should be set for…" he didn't want to finish.

Set for life. Suddenly his horizons felt very small.

But she seemed impressed. "That's amazing. You know how lucky you are, right?"

"I guess so. It seems lame considering what you're doing."

She looked at her feet and when she spoke she was quiet. "My parents took out a second mortgage on our house to get me to NIDA." She swallowed. "They didn't tell me, but I know they did. It's so expensive."

"That's a lot of pressure," Robin said. She nodded. "But they obviously believe in you."

"Yeah."

"Natalie said you were really good."

She shrugged. "I guess I have to be, now."

Buckley reappeared a few minutes later and Evelyn excused herself to use the ladies. Buckley reported that the Candy Bar was packed up and the cash floats were locked away in the safe.

"So how's it going?" Buckley bounced his eyebrows and lowered his voice.

"She's really cool."

"Definitely out of your league. Is she gonna stay over?"

"I hope so," Robin shrugged.

Buckley laughed and poked him in the ribs. "I bet you bloody hope so… here she comes."

Robin heard the door to the ladies swing gently closed. *He knows this place as well as I do.* Evelyn walked up the mezzanine stairs a few moments later with a sickened expression.

"Everything okay?" Robin asked.

She grimaced. "I'd say some poor girl got her period by surprise. It was a bit icky in the end stall."

"Oh," Robin rolled his eyes at Buckley, who was backing away with his hands up, shaking his head. "Maria will sort it out tomorrow."

"Phew!" Buckley flopped in relief. "Thanks, Boss."

Embarrassed, Robin knocked him off for the night. With a big grin for Evelyn and a sly wink for Robin, Buckley pranced through the Cinema Three doors with his sunnies perched on his scalp.

"You lovebirds *behave* now!"

The late shows came out shortly afterwards. Evelyn sat in the foyer while Robin opened the cinema doors and ushered the punters out through the various exits. They were leaving quickly enough, but he was bouncing on his toes all the while. Usually he would give each cinema a superficial clean up after each show, check the exits, empty the bins, spray polish the timber railings… but not tonight.

A guy in his forties spotted the uniform and marched over, frowning. Robin stifled a groan, acutely aware that Evelyn would witness any kind of complaint or confrontation. *What now.*

"Hey excuse me. Hey mate." The guy wore a fluorescently clean white shirt and new looking acid-wash jeans and his hair was slicked back with gel or mousse. "You haven't seen a woman hanging around out here? Yellow top? About my age?"

Robin glanced at Evelyn. She shook her head. "Sorry mate. We've been around all night. Was she meeting you here?"

The bloke pouted. "She met me here before the movie, kind

of for a date, you know? Must've changed her mind."

Evelyn crooned, eyes wide with compassion. Robin gave the bloke a sympathetic shrug.

The bloke sighed and waved a hand. "Never mind. Too bloody skinny for me anyway."

Evelyn barked an outraged laugh and Robin shook his head as the bloke sauntered off.

11

By the time they had the cinema to themselves, it was just after 11pm. Once the taxis cleared away, the scant traffic on Brisbane Street became more or less non-existent and the usual quiet settled over the city.

"Right," Robin clapped his hands. "Sorry that took so long."

"It's okay. I like hanging out here. There's so much… atmosphere."

"Yeah. Every movie kind of has its own vibe too, you can feel it on people when they leave."

"Like they're taking part of it away with them, right? Or maybe leaving part of themselves behind."

"For sure. If it's a good movie, anyway."

"And if it's not?"

"Then they're bitching about the price of the popcorn."

She giggled. "What are we going to watch?"

It was his turn to smile. "Can I show you?"

He led her up the cement stairwell to the top booth. The projector for Cinema One still had its lamp switched on and the audio mixer next to it showed a full array of lights, one for each speaker in the theatre. She pointed to the mixer.

"Why has it got a microphone?"

"That's the intercom system," he said. "For announcements

or emergencies, there are little speakers all through the place."

"Do you ever sing into it, young Robin? When you've got the whole place to yourself?"

He grinned. "Can't say I have, but be my guest, Queen of Speech and Drama."

She giggled. "What *are* we watching?"

"Check this out. When they send us a movie, it comes in separate spools of 35mm film, each one about 20 minutes long. One of my jobs is to splice them together onto a single continuous reel on these feeder plates." He touched one of the three enormous round plates that were attached to the projector. Each plate was roughly the size of a small round dining table. The film itself sat on top of the plates in tightly-wound solid spirals, soothingly neat and somehow crisp. "These reels are the movies – this one is *Space Jam*."

She ran her fingers across the edge of the spool. "All this tape."

"Yeah. The movies all look pretty much the same, depending on how long they run, and the finished plates weigh a bloody ton. But look at this." He touched the middle plate.

"The film's twice as wide."

"That's right. Its seventy-two millimetre film. Pretty much every movie you've ever seen at the cinema has been playing off thirty-five mill. But sometimes – only sometimes, because it's damned expensive – they'll make a seventy-two mill print of a film for festivals or special screenings. Usually it's the big-budget stuff like *Titanic*, or the eye candy documentaries like *Baraka* because the step up in quality is pretty amazing."

"My dad loves *Baraka*," said Evelyn doubtfully.

Robin laughed. "This isn't *Baraka*, but it's the only 72mm film we've got. It was sent to us by mistake and they never asked for it back so…" *I hope I didn't lug this goddamned thing all the way up here for nothing.*

"The suspense is killing me. What is it? *Space Odyssey? Citizen Kane?*"

"Not quite. *Romeo and Juliet.*"

She seized his arm. "Are you joking? The new one? The Baz?"

"You've seen it?"

"Only a dozen times. It's literally my favourite movie." She eyed him suspiciously. "Are you trying to impress me again, young Robin?"

"Trying pretty damned hard, actually."

"*Romeo and Juliet.* What would your Ravenswood mates make of that?"

A laugh fell out of him. "If they've got a problem… well, I simply bite my thumb at them."

"You're a mixed bag," she chuckled. "But I'm not complaining. Do I get an ice cream too?"

"Only if you call it a choc top. Come on."

He took her downstairs to the Candy Bar and they loaded up on snacks. As he was setting two big paper cups underneath the soda taps, she produced a clear glass bottle from her bag. Vodka. Robin added it to both cups.

"It's so quiet now," Evelyn whispered as they went back upstairs to Cinema One. "I can't even hear any cars."

"Yeah. Once the Majestic closes, Launceston's pretty much done for the night. The Royal Oak might still be open but that's four or five blocks away."

"Doesn't it get…I don't know. Lonely?"

"I kinda like it. It feels like you've got the whole town to yourself. Like you could do anything."

He showed her to a seat in the centre of Cinema One, three rows from the back.

"Okay, give me a sec." He ran over to the camouflaged door at the rear of the theatre and propped it open, climbing the short steel ladder that took him into the top booth. The blanket and cushions he had brought down from the Bunker were waiting in a heap next to the projector. The film was loaded and ready to go. He put his hand on the switch.

"Should I start it?" He called. She didn't reply, so he stepped around the projector to look through the window into the theatre.

She wasn't there. He could see their Maltesers and the tops of the vodkas, but not Evelyn.

"Evelyn?" He stepped back and looked along the booth, thinking she may have followed him up the ladder.

She hadn't. He looked back out through the window again, craning his neck. She wasn't in the theatre.

"Evelyn?

Silence. *Maybe she went to the...*

"*Gaaaaaaaah!*"

"*Fuck!*"

She grinned through the window as he stumbled backwards and almost lost his balance. Now she was laughing.

"Jesus." He managed a smile despite the thudding in his chest. "You got me."

She chuckled through the window. "Sorry, couldn't help myse...." She looked away, distracted.

"Should I put the movie on?"

She was frowning into the distance. "Is there somebody else here?"

"Ha, yeah you got me already."

"No, *listen*." She tilted her head. "In there."

He tried to follow her gaze towards the corner of Cinema One. "The Elevator Room?"

"I think there's someone in there."

"I doubt it," he said, grinning. "Those acting skills are pret..."

"No! Listen!"

She stood stock still for a moment, watching him. After a moment she jumped as if goosed and stared at the Elevator room door. "See? Did you hear it?"

"Wait a sec."

He hurried down the ladder and back into the theatre. Evelyn was walking towards the red door and Robin skipped to catch up with her.

"Something was moving in there."

"I hope not. If someone's been stuck in here since the last show..."

He reached the door first and wrenched on the chrome handle, expecting it to swing wide as it had a thousand times before.

It didn't budge. He tried again, but it might as well have been made of stone. He stopped and stood back.

"It's locked." Evelyn said. "Do you have the key?"

"These doors don't have locks or latches. They're the wheelchair exits, they're not allowed to be locked. They *can't* be locked." He tried the door again, but it wouldn't budge.

"Is somebody on the other side?"

"Hello?" Robin called, rapping on the door with a knuckle. "Can you hear us?" There was no reply, so he gripped the door, braced himself, and wrenched at it with all his strength.

The door swung open easily and he barely avoided cracking his own face with it. Once he steadied, he peered into the dark little elevator room. It was empty. He reached in and flicked the light switch, illuminating the red carpeted walls and roof, the silver elevator doors. Empty.

He stepped in and opened the opposite door into Cinema Four. The theatre was dark and still, without the barest stirring of air. He closed the door again and switched off the light in the Elevator Room.

"The door must have been stuck. Another job on the list." He shrugged and gestured to the seats. "Come on, let's watch this thing. It won't seem so quiet in a few minutes."

He trotted back to the booth and raised an eyebrow when Evelyn followed him all the way to the ladder.

"It's a bit... creepy... in here by yourself. The room's so big, but everything seems so... quiet."

"Yep," he called out as he started the projector and checked the audio levels. "It's the acoustic modelling. The carpet on everything, no hard surfaces, sound gets absorbed. You get used to it."

The Cinema One screen flashed to life with a silvery distributor's logo and the atmosphere in the theatre changed as it filled with the movie's presence.

The logo faded to black and an old TV appeared in the middle of the huge screen. There was a brief static of crackle as the TV switched on. A newsreader appeared, all business against a branded blue background, calmly speaking the immortal opening words...

"Two households, both alike in dignity, in fair Verona where we lay our scene..."

A few seconds later *O Verona* blasted out from the Dolby surround sound system, shaking the walls and seats. The fast cuts and sweeping zooms of the film's booming prologue made the familiar goose bumps flush along Robin's forearms.

As the music swelled and pulled them into a world of Mexican pastiche Shakespeare could never have imagined, Evelyn grabbed Robin's forearm and pulled him closer. He didn't mind at all. They settled in.

It was about an hour later, as Romeo exited Verona in the sunrise, that the banging started.

12

Robin recognised the sound immediately; somebody was rattling on the glass doors at the front entrance, trying to get in to the foyer.

"They just want to use the toilet," Robin said. "They'll give up in a sec."

Evelyn nodded and eased back into his side... then sat bolt upright as the banging started again, much louder and much closer. Now it was coming from the Cinema One street exit, an unmarked door just a few metres up Brisbane Street from the main entrance.

"Persistent," Robin frowned. "Usually they don't realise that exit door is..."

"*Evelyn? Evelyn!*" It was a young woman's voice.

"Oh." Evelyn was biting her lips, clearly fighting a grin.

"You know who that is?" Robin asked.

"*Evelyyyn!*"

"It's my friend Diana. And probably her boyfriend." She shrugged. "I told her I was coming here and... she kinda didn't believe me... so..."

"Right."

"You're annoyed."

"No. No, of course not, it's fine."

She put her arms around his neck. "They won't stay all night… but… *I* might. If that's okay?" Robin leaned in to kiss her, but before he could, the banging started again.

"EVELYYYYYN…."

They went down the short set of stairs next to the screen that led to Cinema One's bottom exit. Robin heard a muffled voice outside - *"I told you she was full of it"* – and pushed the door open with a loud rattle.

"Oh!" The girl standing just outside the door jumped back and knocked into her boyfriend, who caught her and then took a step to steady himself. They looked at Robin, unsure. "Sorry, we were looking for…uh…"

"For a good time love?" Evelyn stepped out from behind Robin, grinning. The girl – Diana presumably – squealed and leapt upon her friend. They hugged and laughed hello, talking over the top of each other.

The boyfriend, Steven, was dressed in an op-shop suit probably more suited to his great-grandfather. As the girls embraced, he caught Robin's eye and nodded in greeting and the two young men shared a moment of instant camaraderie; *Hey buddy, how fuckin' lucky are we?*

Robin extended a hand. "Robin."

"Steven." They shook.

"Come in, come in."

"Are you sure?" Diana asked loudly. "Can we really? You're not gonna get in trouble?"

"Its fine," Robin told her. Evelyn nodded enthusiastically.

He led them back up the stairs into Cinema One, then up the steel ladder into the top booth.

"That's some pretty impressive kit," Steven offered, checking out the projectors.

Robin turned down the volume in Cinema One. Juliet was glaring out of the screen, her face coated in brightly dripping blood, her wrists bound in iron chains. Robin had watched *Romeo and Juliet* more than once, but he didn't recognise the scene. *Must be the director's cut*, he thought dismissively.

"Cinema One has the best sound system. It was installed at the same time as Cinema Four, but it's twice the size." The movie would need to play through until it wound down and switched off automatically. Stopping the reel mid-spool was a risky business even with 35mm film. With 72 mill, he would be asking for trouble.

"It's weird seeing the place so empty," Steven looked out the projectionist's window, his voice hushed. "Kind of creepy."

"*You're* kind of creepy," Evelyn teased and he rolled his eyes.

"Do you really live up here?" Diana asked Robin. She was unsteady on her feet, but doing a good job of managing it.

"Yeah. Well. Not here. Come upstairs and I'll show you."

"What about the movie?" Evelyn asked. She was biting her lip, unsure of his mood.

He smiled and pecked her on the cheek. "We can watch it again sometime?"

"Oh shit. We're totally intruding." Diana pulled at Steven's lapel. "We brought rum though."

Steven produced an unopened bottle of dark rum from inside his coat and wiggled it at Robin. Diana waved her hands around it, big smile, jazz fingers. Evelyn was biting her bottom lip. The three of them watched Robin, waiting for his reaction.

He laughed at their expressions. "Come on then. Let's get fucked up."

They cheered and followed him up the cement stairwell, their footsteps echoing through the building.

13

They pulled up around his squat wooden coffee table. Steven and Diana took a fat armchair at each end of it while Robin and Evelyn flopped back into the old Chesterfield.

"How the fuck did they get that couch up here?" Steven mused as he poured four thick lines of rum into the glasses Robin had produced. "It looks a hundred years old."

"No idea," Robin admitted. "This building's been a theatre since the 1880's I think. So it's probably been here a while."

"Do your parents own this place?" Diana asked.

"My uncle. He's training me up to run it."

"So it could all be yours one day when he croaks?" Steven asked, handing Robin a rum and coke.

"Steven!" Diana frowned.

Robin shrugged, uncomfortable. "He keeps pretty fit. He'll probably outlive me by decades."

"His uncle's cool, Steven." Evelyn said, leaning back into Robin and squeezing his thigh.

Steven put his hands up in defence. "All right, Jesus, sorry. Just making conversation." He rolled his eyes.

"Did you go to Launceston College, Robin?" Diana asked.

"No, no LC for me," Robin smiled at her. "Is that how you

guys met?"

"It's how we all met," she beamed at Evelyn. "Skipping class and drinking Passion Pop in Royal Park. And they say education separates us from the beasts." Her eyes rolled, then suddenly went wide and she grabbed Evelyn by the wrist. "Oh my *god*. You're *never* going to believe who's pregnant!"

For a while they talked about people Robin didn't know. Steven finished his drink almost immediately, so Robin downed his as well.

Instant party, Robin thought, pleased. He liked having people over at the Bunker, though on the rare occasion it happened it was usually his old mates from Ravenswood or Karoola. While Steven was refilling their drinks and the girls were discussing the relative merits of the Red Cross Op Shop, Robin went over and knelt next to his white cupboard. Wriggling and yanking, he pulled an entire drawer out of the sideboard and carried it back to the table.

"Check this out," he told them, shifting their glasses to make room for the drawer.

"What. The. Fuck." There was awe in Steven's voice.

"Oh my god, Robin," Diana shuffled forward in her chair, peering into the drawer with wide eyes.

"Some of it was confiscated," Robin mused, holding up a small bag of weed. "Most of it we just find on the floor."

There were other bags of weed in the drawer and more; a couple of dozen pills in a variety of shapes and colours, three or four gram bags lined with white or yellowish powder, a sandwich bag holding oddly serrated squares of thin cardboard, a black leather purse. And cigarettes, so many cigarettes; 20 packs, 50s, pouches, papers, filters, the lot.

"Jesus," Steven breathed, his eyes bright. "You're a fucking apothecary."

Robin nodded. "I'm not really into any of it, but I smoke a little doobie from time to time. Maybe I should roll us one?"

"Do you have a bong?" Steven sat forward. Robin shook his head and Steven sat back again.

"You should let Steven roll it," Diana confided. "He makes amazing joints." Her boyfriend was nodding, so Robin handed it over.

"Be my guest."

"What's this?" Evelyn asked. She was waving a clear sandwich bag that held several pieces of cardboard. Each was the size of a credit card, printed with what appeared to be rows of smiley faces.

"Acid," Diana told her. "Enough acid for a small music festival."

"Can you overdose on acid?"

"I'm not sure," Steven said, his fingers busy with weed. "Wanna find out?" They all laughed.

Steven did roll a good joint; this one was smooth and missile-shaped with a perfect twist at the end. He offered to Robin.

"Do the honours, sir?"

"Why thank you good sir." Using one of the lighters from the drawer, Robin sparked up the joint. Sweetly acrid smoke drifted lazily through the Bunker. "Nicely done."

He took another puff and passed it to Evelyn, who barely brushed her lips on it before passing it on to Diana. Diana settled back into her chair with it, taking a long, comfortable drag.

Evelyn leaned over the drawer again, rifling through the eclectic stash.

"So many lighters. Oh. Look at this." She fished a piece of

folded cardboard out of the drawer and Robin felt the hair on his arms stand up.

"The Ruby Club. Only one match has been used." Evelyn turned the matchbook this way and that. "It looks like blood."

Robin smiled half-heartedly. "I thought that too. I found it downstairs a few months ago."

"Kinky," Steven chuckled. "It looks like it's from a strip club."

Diana rolled her eyes. "As if, it's like a hundred year old."

"Naked ladies and red curtains? The Ruby Club? It *has* to be a strip club. Or a brothel."

"Creepy," Evelyn frowned, sitting the matchbook back in the drawer.

Steven snatched it up. "Look, it's the same red as the curtains that are all through this place."

"Those curtains are in every cinema everywhere," Robin said.

"He said that this place has been a theatre for a hundred years," Steven nodded at Robin. "Maybe it was a strip club at some point too."

"Maybe your grandmother worked there," Evelyn suggested.

Steven pushed the matchbox against his nostril sand inhaled deeply, with satisfaction. "Ah. Smells like sexy nannas."

Evelyn and Robin groaned, while Diana screeched and whacked him in the arm.

"Oh bloody hell Steven," Evelyn rolled her eyes.

"Yeah you can keep that," Robin was shaking his head, smirking.

Steven grinned and gave Robin the thumbs up. "Cheers bro, I'll use it wisely." He sniffed the matchbox again with exaggerated pleasure, then slipped it into his pocked looking pleased.

Diana pouted. "Of course, anything to do with a bloody strip club gets you all excited…" Steven laughed and tickled her and she collapsed and cosied into him.

"I love the posters in here so much," Evelyn told them, standing up. "Some of them go back to the forties too."

"*A Clockwork Orange,*" Diana said. "That's wicked. And *Lost Highway.*"

"I put that one up," Robin told her. "I've only added a couple though. Last year when I was cleaning up the Ticket Box I found that *Young Einstein* one. It's signed by Yahoo Serious."

"Oh god I forgot that movie," Steven laughed, waving the joint like a sceptre. "Einstein in Tasmania. And he invents beer."

"That's the one."

"This is amazing." Evelyn was looking at a large, faded lithograph, mostly composed of a mottled charcoal background that was probably jet black once. Standing bright against all the gloom was Rita Hayworth, resplendent in an aqua and lavender evening gown, a perfectly poised cigarette leaking smoke into the negative space. Although the text has faded with the years, Rita has somehow kept her vibrancy. "*Gilda.* She's so elegant."

With a subtle shift in her shoulders and a long slow breath, Evelyn moved her body to match Rita Hayworth's pose. With her eyes lidded, lips pouting and a delicate hand holding an invisible cigarette, the resemblance was uncanny.

"Nailed it," chuckled Steven.

"This girl," Diana shook Robin's knee, "*my* Evelyn, is gonna win an Oscar one day. Guarantee it."

"I believe it," Robin said, and he did, if her imitation of the poster was anything to go by anyway.

Evelyn blushed and relaxed. "It's a cool poster."

Robin took a longer, slower drag this time around. The joint was almost finished. "There are more. Down in the workshop there's a couple of storage cupboards full of old stuff. David never really bothered cleaning the place out."

"More posters?" Evelyn asked.

"I'm pretty sure."

"More drugs?" Steven said hopefully. Diana laughed.

They shared another round of drinks and Steven helped himself to a cigarette from the drawer. The weed made the air in the bunker soft and sleepy and before long, Evelyn was nuzzling into Robin's neck on the stiff Chesterfield. It was... nice.

Diana had climbed into Steven's lap and they were whispering to each other, giggling. After a while she sat up, straightening up her sleeves. "Um, Robin... where could a girl use the bathroom?"

Robin blinked, lazy. "There's a little loo down in the bottom booth, but the women's in the foyer is probably... cleaner." He could feel Evelyn smiling against the skin of his throat.

Diana snorted. "I might go down to the ladies. Is that okay?"

"Mi casa, su casa."

"Come on," Diana pulled Steven to his feet. He stretched as he stood up, his crumpled op-shop shirt riding up to reveal his bony hips and the tattered waistband of his Bonds underwear.

"Just follow the stairs down. The lights should all be on." Robin waved them away. Diana was giggling and leaning on Steven for support as they exited the Bunker.

Robin ran a finger across Evelyn's cheek. "Hmm. Would you like another drink?"

She raised her head to look at him, her eyes shining and her cheeks flushed.

"No. There's something else I want, young Robin." She kissed him, her thigh drifting up to rest across his stomach. "Young, *cock* Robin."

He gave her what she wanted.

14

Sometime later Robin rolled off his mattress and pulled his work pants back on. Evelyn was dozing underneath his doona with one slender ankle poking out.

Amazing. I could get used to this. He was pleasantly woozy from the booze and weed and sex. *But I won't. Because she's leaving.*

He saw that she was watching him watching her and smiled, swooping back in for a kiss. She was bed warm and bed fuzzy.

"I gotta go pee," he whispered in his best Forrest Gump voice.

She snorted. "Oh god me too. Take me with you?"

"Of course, m'lady."

While she fished around for her underwear, Robin poured a fresh rum and coke – more coke than rum, this time – and drained half of it in a gulp.

"Which way? It's so *quiet* up here." She stood next to him and his mouth was suddenly dry again.

In the muted light of the bunker, dressed only in her underwear, hair hanging loose around her shoulders... *she's pure Hollywood.* He shook his head in wonder, drinking in the sight of her.

She frowned. "What?"

He laughed and pulled her on to his lap. "You... are fucking gorgeous." He kissed her and she pulled him tight. "You'll be on a poster up here one day. Launceston's Rita Heyworth."

She rolled her eyes and pulled away. "And you'll have a wet knee if you don't show me where this toilet is."

They left the bunker and walked down the cemented steps to the top booth. Evelyn used the little bathroom at the far end of the booth – "There's a *shower* in here!" – while Robin fussed in the kitchenette. He opened a bag of Doritos and some basil dip, arranging them on one of the old wooden trays he used to carry food up to his bunker.

Evelyn came out of the bathroom looking somehow fresher and more arranged despite the fact she was still in her underwear.

"Oh this looks good," she said, pressing into him.

"It's not the only thing."

"Should we take it up to the…"

A scream, a woman's scream, loud and terrified. It sliced through the darkness, piercing the quiet of the cinema.

Robin's blood ran cold. Evelyn clutched at him.

Another scream came, even louder, gratingly loud, too loud.

Evelyn clapped her hands to her ears, her eyes horrified. "Diana!"

"The foyer, come on!" Robin took her by the wrist. He glanced up at the sensor panel as they ran towards the door - the <u>Foyer</u> and <u>Cinema Three</u> lights were blinking steadily. All the others were dark.

Another scream, guttural and despairing, made Robin wince as he led Evelyn down the cement stairs. They dashed through the storeroom and into the foyer, looking around wildly. Nothing moved, not even the posters hanging from the foyer ceiling.

"Diana!" Evelyn yelped. "Diana, where are you?"

"They must have gone into one of the cinemas," Robin muttered.

"Diana! Steven!"

"Should I call the..."

The Cinema Three doors creaked.

Robin and Evelyn spun to watch them slowly swing open – and Diana's face popped out, her hair mussed, her cheeks flushed, and her eyes bright.

"What's going on," she blinked. "Are you going home, Evelyn?"

"Are you okay?" Evelyn skipped over to her and Robin followed. "Why were you screaming?"

"Screaming?" Diana giggled. "I don't think so... was I screaming?"

"Maybe a bit." Steven appeared behind her, buckling his jeans up. He put a hand on Diana's waist and she elbowed him in the ribs. He grinned at Robin, but his eyes widened when he saw Evelyn standing there in her underwear.

"No it was like... *screaming* screaming," Evelyn told them. "Didn't you hear it?"

"We might have been... busy..." Steven's voice was dry.

Evelyn shook her head and looked at Robin for support. "You heard it."

He was already nodding. "I definitely heard it. It was *so* loud. And it was coming from here, from the foyer. You *must* have heard it."

Their faces were blank.

Robin walked over to the Candy Bar and peered across the counter, but nobody was hiding in the serving area.

"Maybe it was someone outside," Steven suggested.

"No, it wasn't," Evelyn said, looking nervously up at the front entrance.

Steven shrugged, his eyes flitting from her underwear, to her bra, to her legs and back again.

"None of the other doors are unlocked," Robin told them as he came back down stairs. *None except...* he looked at the Control Room door. *No, it has to be locked.*

They watched him swallow and reluctantly approach the door.

"Robin?" Evelyn called. He didn't answer.

It can't be unlocked, he thought as he reached for the Control Room door.

But it was. Of course it was. It opened easily. The light was on. The low, mechanical hum of the air conditioning had a chanting quality. He clicked the door open, then stepped across the threshold, steeling himself to look around the corner. The others still watched him.

He took a deep breath... and looked.

There was nothing. Just a little cement room with a high ceiling. The AC unit ticked away as usual and the only other sound was the faintest dripping.

Dripping? Robin frowned and walked towards the control panel. *If the air conditioner is leaking water then the whole...*

"Help me."

He froze. The voice was barely a whisper, but he heard it clearly. A young woman's voice. The voice he had heard just before... just before...

"Please." The voice was coming from the air conditioner, from the row of small vents just below the control panel.

Impossible. Robin swallowed, throat dry and hands trembling. "Hello?"

"Take me away from here."

"Where…" he licked his lips. They felt like paper. "Where *are* you? How can…"

"They won't let me leave." The voice was a sob now.

Something touched Robin's shoulder. Gasping, he stumbled back against the concrete wall, brushing madly at his shoulder. *Blood.* It had dripped onto him from above.

The spot on the wall he had cleaned just hours earlier, the spot he had scrubbed until his fingers hurt, was now a gaping, fleshy wound. Blood so thick and dark that it glugged liked ichor coated the wall below the wound, but the mess ran *up* the wall, defying gravity, as though the wound was sucking the gore back into itself. Slow streams, thin rivulets and sluggish globules, stinking of meat and rotting earth, eased up the wall and disappeared into the infected opening.

He didn't want to look at it. It didn't make sense. *I cleaned it up already.* The stench was unbearable.

"They won't let me leave." A pulse of bile oozed into the wound, trailing lumps of putrescence.

Robin backed away towards the Control Room door. He kept his eyes on the bloody mess until the very last moment, and when he ducked around the corner he scrambled to open the Control Room door, which – to his blessed relief – pulled open easily in his shaking hand.

With the door slammed closed behind him, Robin put his hands on his knees and let out a long, shaky breath. His stomach was gurgling and his mouth was watering in a way that only happened just before he…

I'm not gonna throw up. He gulped another shuddering breath. *I'm not gonna throw up.*

"What the actual fuck," said Diana. The three of them were

watching him, their faces aghast. Evelyn unfroze first. She ran to him and made him stand up straight.

"What happened? What's in there?" She looked at the Control Room door, fear and confusion plain on her face.

"It was… nothing. I just…"

Steven scowled at him. "Bullshit." He strode over to the Control Room door.

"No!"

"Steven, what are you doing?" Diana squealed. "Don't go in there!"

Steven grabbed the Control Room door handle and pulled.

It didn't budge. Or twist. He rattled it in frustration. "You locked it. What's in there, Robin?"

"I didn't lock it," Robin said. His breath was coming back, his stomach settling. "I just pulled it shut."

"Well unlock it!"

"I can't. My keys…"

"This is creeping me the fuck out," Diana declared, hands up. "I want to go, Steven."

"Babe, he's just messing around…"

"I don't *care,* I want to *go!*"

Evelyn put an arm around her friend. "Let's go back upstairs. Your stuff's up there anyway." Diana let Evelyn lead her to the Candy Bar door.

The boys followed them in to the storeroom, but as they reached the cement stairwell Steven pulled on Robin's elbow, shaking him from his daze.

"Was it the rat?" Steven demanded quietly.

"Excuse me?"

"It was the rat, right? I can understand why you wouldn't wanna say in front of the girls, but I think you might have freaked them out anyway."

Help me.

"We don't have rats in the cinema."

Steven scoffed. "Of course you do."

Robin pulled his arm free. "We don't. The building's sealed along all sides, there's nowhere for rats to get in."

They won't let me leave.

"Of course you've got a bloody rat," Steven laughed. "It was crawling around the floor the whole bloody time we were in the cinema. The size of a fucking dog, it sounded like."

"Let's go upstairs," Robin told him.

15

Diana was sitting on the Chesterfield, cradling a drink and a cigarette. Steven flopped down next to her and stretched along the couch, his eyes following Evelyn. Still in her knickers, she was rummaging around on Robin's bed.

Robin examined the sensor board – it was dark. Maybe the screaming *had been* outside. He shook his head to clear it.

Evelyn found a white *Metallica* t-shirt in one of Robin's drawers and pulled it on. Steven sighed in disappointment, probably thinking nobody noticed... but they all did. Evelyn smoothed the t-shirt over her hips and sat on one of the huge armchairs, crossing her legs. *And Justice for all,* the shirt proclaimed.

"Should we have another joint?" Steven asked nobody in particular. Nobody answered. The drawer was still sitting on the coffee table, so he helped himself.

"What was in that room?" Evelyn asked Robin as he sat down heavily in the other armchair.

"I... it was a rat." Robin lied.

Steven coughed and shook his head.

Evelyn frowned. "A rat? Really? You looked so... shaken up."

Robin smiled and hoped it didn't look as sick as he felt. "We don't get many rats here." He didn't look at Steven. "They made a real mess."

"And the screaming?" Evelyn insisted.

Robin opened his mouth, realised he didn't have an answer, and closed it again.

"It was out on the street," Steven said firmly. "The Royal Oak would still be open. Just some pissed kids on the way home."

"No." Evelyn shook her head. "It wasn't somebody having fun."

"Can you just stop talking about it?" Diana had finished her cigarette and she reached for another one. "I think that weed made me paranoid."

"Better have some more then," Steven chuckled, holding up the bomber joint he had just finished rolling. He puffed it alight, then offered it to his girlfriend.

"No thanks," Diana muttered.

When Robin and Evelyn both shook their heads as well, Steven shrugged.

"Fuck it, more for me then."

Thick smoke drifted through the Bunker, pungent in the small space. Evelyn coughed.

"Can you put some music on?" Diana suggested.

"For sure," Robin stood up and flicked on the little stereo that sat on the floor next to his TV. Tinny beats filled the space, fighting against the oppressive mood. "City Park FM play some decent stuff this time of the morning."

Steven took a big drag and offered the joint around again. Still no takers. "I left my shoes down there." He grinned at Robin. "Think the rat will eat them?"

"Not bloody likely," Diana muttered. Steven frowned at her.

"Can I put something on?" Evelyn asked Robin quietly,

nodding at the stereo. He smiled gently.

She reached across the table and twisted the stereo's tuner, looking for a station, her head down. As she twisted and listened, the hem of the Metallica t-shirt drifted up to her lower back.

Eyes locked on Evelyn's panties, Steven eased back onto the couch and sighed contentedly, making no effort to hide his appreciation. Diana whacked her boyfriend's chest with the back of her hand.

"What the fuck, Steven," she demanded.

"What?" He grinned, smug.

"Stop staring at her ass!" She spat.

Steven winced. Evelyn quickly sat back in her chair, pulling the t-shirt down, blushing furiously.

"What are you talking about," Steven muttered, his own cheeks flushed.

"You've been staring at her ever since we came out of the cinema. Why Steven?" Her lips quivered dangerously as she turned to face him on the couch. "Do you want to fuck her?"

"Diana…" Evelyn's voice was soft as she looked askance at her friends.

"Well, do you?" Diana stood up, fists on her hips, seething with fury. "*Do* you want to *fuck* this girl, Sam?"

"What the hell, Diana," Steven stood up as well, his eyes fiery. "What are you doing?"

"Just tell me! Do you?" She pushed his shoulder, a short, sharp jab.

"Hey hey…" Robin stood up slowly, looking back and forth between them.

"Don't fucking touch me!" Steven spat.

"Why do you keep looking at her? I'm not enough for you

anymore?"

Evelyn was holding her face in her hands.

Steven glanced at her, then sneered at his girlfriend. "Look at her. Look what she's fucking wearing. Sorry Evelyn but… of course I'm gonna fucking look. What do you expect?"

Robin spoke up at that. "Okay mate. I think it might be time to call it a night."

Steven gaped at him, incredulous. "You're kicking me out? You want *me* to leave?"

Robin held his hands up, palms open, like David had taught him. "It's been a great night and I liked meeting you both… but we're all drunk and stoned. It's late. Let's call it."

"I'm not going with him." Diana had her arms crossed. Evelyn stood and hugged her friend and Diana leaned into her.

"Diana," Steven said through gritted teeth. "You're staying at my house."

"Not anymore," she said. "My parent's think I'm at Evelyn's anyway."

"So what, you wanna stay here?" Steven sneered.

"She'll be fine, Steven. Call her tomorrow when you're both sober," Evelyn reasoned.

"Don't fucking bother," Diana muttered.

Steven stared at Diana. "You're actually gonna stay at this guy's place. While he kicks *me* out." She didn't respond, so he glared at Robin, who shrugged and crossed his arms. "Oh good on you, you smug prick."

"Steven just go," Evelyn and Diana said it together.

Steven reeled back, as if slapped, his mouth working. Finally the words came.

"Fuck the lot of you then." He turned on his heel and marched towards the Bunker door. "Enjoy your goddamned threesome!"

He kicked Robin's bin over as he passed, sending bottles and takeaway containers clattering across the floor with a waft of beer and soy sauce. Then he was gone.

"Shit." Robin quickly pulled a t-shirt on.

"Just let him go Robin," Evelyn shook her head.

"I can't. If he trashes the booth..." He followed Steven out of the Bunker with Evelyn and Diana right behind him.

As Robin dashed down the stairwell, he heard Steven close the bottom booth door and swore. *Just go down the stairs, you wanker.* He reached the door a moment later and yanked it open.

The elevator door was just closing. Robin ran over to it and looked in through the little glass window, the girls crowding his shoulder.

Steven was leaning against the elevator wall. When he saw their faces looking in at him, he sneered and gave them the finger. The elevator began to move.

"Fucking tool," Diana muttered. "What the..."

Steven was unzipping his fly. He gave Robin a sly grin.

"*No,* don't you fucking *dare*..." Robin shouted.

They heard Steven laughing as he dropped out of sight.

Robin groaned. "Jesus, he won't *piss* in there, will he?" When Diana didn't answer, Robin swore again and ran for the door. "Come on, the elevator's slow, we'll beat him down by a mile."

He led them down the cement stairwell into the Candy Bar. Robin could hear the elevator descending, the subtle hum in the walls. They reached the chrome doors near the Cinema Four entrance a few moments later.

"If he's pissed in there, he'll be cleaning it up," Robin said to Diana. She just nodded.

They heard the elevator settle into place. Robin steeled

himself for a confrontation as the doors slid open.

But the elevator was empty. There was no sign of Steven.

"What the fuck?" Robin dropped his hands.

"Where is he?" Evelyn asked. Robin blinked at her. "Did he stop at another floor?"

"There *are* no other floors." Robin said, his mouth dry.

Diana pulled away from Evelyn and peered at Robin. "What do you mean? Where did he go then?"

"There's nowhere for the elevator to stop between the booth and here. He couldn't have gotten out."

"Then he must have gotten back out in the booth! Come on!" She waited for him to move, but Robin is shaking his head.

"We watched him go down. You can't stop the lift once it starts. He had to come out here. There's nowhere else to go."

Diana and Evelyn stared at him. The elevator clicked and the door began to slide shut again, but Robin put an arm out to stop it.

Evelyn looked into the little elevator. Its burnished steel walls were almost seamless, except for the doors and the round, numbered buttons. Even the roof was a solid sheet of metal.

"I thought maybe... in the movies, they always get into the elevator shaft through the ceiling..."

Robin grimaced. "He's not Bruce Willis. And anyway, there's no manhole."

Diana's lip is trembling. "Then, where the *fuck* is he, Robin? Where did he go?"

I don't know.

"Come on," Evelyn put her hands on Diana's shoulders. "Let's go back upstairs. He probably just went back up to get his rum."

"I'll keep looking around," Robin said. "If he's up there, just call out. I'll hear you."

Evelyn nodded and led Diana towards the Cinema One doors. "Can we go this way? Up the ladder?"

Robin nodded. "It's still unlocked. Just… be careful in the booth, okay?"

Evelyn nodded again and they went.

The elevator doors began to close again and this time Robin let them. Moving quickly, he did a circuit of the foyer, checking every door and nook. Ticket Box, staff room, gents, cleaning cupboard, ladies, Candy Bar, David's office. All clear. The only places left to check were the theatres… and the Control Room. *Not in there. Not again.*

Reluctantly, slowly, he tried the Control Room door. The handle moved easily. *It was locked when Steven tried to open it.* He set his jaw and pushed, torch in hand.

The lights were still on. The air conditioner hummed its monotonous tone. He snuck in without a sound, without a breath, steeling himself for blood, for Steven slumped on the floor.

Or bashing into the goddamned roof…

The room was empty. There was no blood, not even a dark patch where the stain had once been.

Just seeing things. Robin swallowed, flinching at the loud click in his dry throat. *I imagined it. All of it.* He backed out of the room, feeling lightheaded. *Then where is he?*

When the door to the Control Room was shut, his breath came back in a great gush. *Goddamn it.* He strode back through the foyer, then stopped, considering the glass doors of the front entrance. Steven could have let himself out that way - the front doors would open even if they were locked on the outside, you just had to push them. One might still be ajar.

He started on the left side and worked his way along, pushing each of the glass doors to make sure they were solidly locked. They all were. When he reached the last door he leaned into it instead, gazing out into Brisbane Street.

No movement around the pub or the lolly shop. Robin peered down the street towards the TasMilk depot, then checked the dark crannies along the side of the big department store for any movement. Just as he was about to turn away he heard heavy footsteps on the footpath outside.

Here he comes, Robin thought as a man walked into view – but it wasn't Steven. Just some drunk bloke in an oversized khaki jacket stomping his way towards the mall.

The drunk glanced into the foyer and kept shuffling... then stopped again, pulling up just outside the glass doors.

Wavering like a sailor too long at sea, the drunk was grinning at something in the foyer. He tilted two fingers in a friendly greeting and dropped a sly wink.

He's waving to his own reflection, thought Robin. *Damn, I wish I was that drunk.*

The bloke abruptly seemed to notice Robin standing there and he took an unsteady step back – then threw back his head and roared laughter. His voice was deep and booming and rich. Robin couldn't help but grin at him through the glass. The drunk kept laughing, holding his belly, until he stumbled a few steps towards the door where Robin was standing.

"Sorry bruv, sorry bruv, I didn't see you there," he laughed again. Robin could see spit on his chin. "That's a good lookin woman you've got yourself, brother, do you mind if I say *hello?*" He laughed again, nasty this time.

Robin frowned over his shoulder at the empty foyer. "Evelyn? Diana?" There was nobody there.

"Wanna come and get a drink sweetheart?"

Robin scowled. "Who do you think you're you talking to mate?"

The drunk sneered. "Yer missus mate. Doesn't look like you can handle her."

Surveying the mezzanine, Robin shined his Maglite's white beam into the dim corners.

The drunk ignored him. "Come on gorgeous, how about you come and…" he stepped back abruptly, his cheeks slack and his eyes wide.

Robin shined the torch on the man's disbelieving face.

"…and… what in the name of god…" the drunk backed away. His big boots tangled and he fell back, landing on his ass, but his eyes never left the space next to Robin's shoulder.

Robin felt fear bloom in his chest. He turned his head slowly, feeling the tendons creak.

There was nothing there.

The drunk was gasping for breath, kicking his feet, trying to push himself backwards, trying to get away, horror plain on his face.

Robin's own breath was coming fast and cold. "What is it?" His voice was shrill. "What *is it? What can you see?*"

The drunk tore his gaze away and his hysterical eyes settled on Robin. Panting, the drunk clambered to his feet, awkwardly clutching at his left shoulder.

"*Wait, tell me!*"

The drunk turned and ran, his left arm hanging uselessly by his side. After five steps, he was out of sight.

Robin was frozen to the spot. His breath came fast and heavy. *Move,* he told himself.

The mezzanine was silent again. He could almost hear his own heartbeat.

Move. There was nothing there. You're not a child.

The drunk had been looking at the space right next to him.

Move. The girls are still upstairs.

That did it. He turned and ran to the Candy Bar door without looking back.

16

"Something isn't right." Robin tried to stop the panic from squeezing his voice.

Evelyn and Diana were sitting together on the Chesterfield, both with damp eyes and red cheeks. Diana was sniffling, looking down at the floor, but Evelyn frowned up at him.

"What do you mean?"

"I mean… I think we should get out of here. Something isn't right." *Christ, you sound insane.*

"Did you find him?" Diana asked, her voice thick. She still didn't look up.

"I… no."

"Then shouldn't we keep looking him?" Evelyn asked. "What if he's hurt? Or trapped somewhere?"

Diana hiccupped and sobbed. "So fucking what. He's always so *sleazy* around you, Evelyn!"

Robin swallowed. *Tell them. Tell them.*

"Diana," his voice was even. "When you and Steven were in Cinema Three…"

"We were fucking. Well… he tried to, but…"

"Did you hear anything while you were in there?"

"What are you talking about, Robin?"

"Steven told me that he heard a noise in there, something on the floor." They were both staring at him. *I'm babbling.* "Did you hear anything?"

After a moment she nodded. *"He* said it sounded like a rat. But it didn't."

"Then what?"

She hesitated again. "I thought it was a movie playing in one of the other rooms... or... I don't know, the air conditioner..."

"What did it sound like?"

She looked at Evelyn, then at the floor. "It sounded like crying."

"Crying?" Evelyn said softly. "We heard screaming."

Diana shook her head. "I never heard that. It was quiet, like muffled. But not screaming, just... what difference does it make anyway?"

Tell them. But Robin struggled to find the words. *They'll think you've lost it.* He shivered. *Maybe you have.*

"It doesn't make any difference. We should just go." He sat down on the bed to pull his shoes on and Evelyn came over and sat beside him.

"Robin," her voice was low. "You're scaring me."

He stopped fiddling with his laces and put an arm around her. She tensed, but didn't shrug his arm away.

"I'm sorry. I just... I don't think it's safe here."

She glanced at Diana, who still hadn't moved. Her voice was low. "Steven's random, but he's not *violent.* He's not going to *attack* us or anyth..."

"It's not Steven I'm worried about," he said, blunter than he intended.

"Is there someone else here?" Her fingernails dug into his arm.

"I don't know. Maybe. There's been… I think we just need to go."

She stared at him but he didn't know what else to say. After a moment she nodded anyway.

"Right. We'll go through Cinema One and down the stairs to the exit, the same way you came in."

"Why not the main entrance?"

Because something's there. Robin shook his head "The Cinema One exit is closest."

He led them out of the Bunker and down the echoing stairwell. Somewhere deep in the belly of the building, the air conditioner churned. Once they were in the top booth, they huddled in the kitchenette next to Robin's abandoned tray of snacks.

"The ladder up the end," he whispered. "Then back down through Cinema One, the way you came in… wait!"

They stopped as he peered through the projectionist's window into Cinema One. The house lights were on, but dim. The theatre was silent. The only movement was the steam drifting down from the air conditioners. He looked back at the sensor panel above the door. The lights were all off.

"All right, let's go." They descended the short ladder and stood together in the closet-sized landing, the girls eyeing each other. He put a hand on the door into Cinema One and steeled himself.

"Just follow me. Don't stop. Okay?"

Evelyn nodded but Diana just frowned at him.

"Okay." The door opened with a reluctant creak. He eased through, Evelyn right at his shoulder.

Jesus! The air in the theatre hit his face with an icy slap. *It's freezing in here!*

The carpet crunched under Robin's foot. Even in the dim light, he could see the soft glinting of ice on the carpeted walls and the top of the seats, the frost on the steel hand railings, the steam pouring from the air conditioners...

"Oh it's so *cold!*" Diana squealed.

"It's all frozen," Evelyn wondered, pulling the puffer jacket tight.

"The air conditioners." Robin sucked in a breath and it burned his throat. "Someone... some*thing*... is fucking with them. Let's get out of here."

Evelyn grabbed his arm. "Wait. Listen." Her words drifting to steam as soon as they left her lips.

There was a rattling sound in the other back corner of the theatre. The door to the Elevator Room. Another rattle... then a heavy thud made it jump.

"Come on!" Robin's voice was shrill, his heart thumping.

He sprinted down the aisle, holding his breath against the painfully chilly air. When he reached the slippery, frosty stairs he skittled down them, holding the icy hand rail for balance.

A line of warm, yellow light was glowing at the bottom of the exit door from the streetlight outside. He threw himself at it and when his feet slipped on the last few treacherous steps he slammed into the door with his entire body, pushing it against the latch, opening it the barest inch for the barest second.

A sliver of warm night air caressed his cheek.

The exit! Flooded with adrenaline and relief, Robin seized the door handle ready to lunge into the warm night air, but he looked over his shoulder and his relief shattered.

Neither Evelyn nor Diana had followed him. They weren't at the exit, weren't on the stairs.

"Come *on!*" He roared at the stairs, bouncing on his toes.

"Let's *go!*"

He turned the handle – it turned so *easily* - and went to push the door wide open...

"Evelyn!" Diana shrieked. *"Stop!"*

Go. Just go! Robin's hand tightened on the cold handle. *Just open the door and you're out! Just go!*

"Evelyn!" Diana's voice was ripe with fear. "Evelyn *don't!"*

"Fuck!" Letting the door handle go, Robin turned and ran back up the stairs, his shoes slipping on the ice.

The red-walled theatre was now a mottled grey. Sparkling frost drifted down from the roof in frozen clouds. A fine white fog was gathering beneath the seats, shifting and growing, pulsing with breath. Robin was careful to avoid it as he ran back up the aisle's gentle slope.

At the back of the theatre, only a few metres from the camouflaged door they had come through, Diana crouched on the floor. Her arms were wrapped around her knees and her breath steamed around her ears, her shoulders hitching and shaking.

Robin ran straight past her and sprinted towards Evelyn, who had almost reached the door of the Elevator Room. She moved languorously, as if in a frozen dream.

What the hell is she doing?

"Evelyn!" Robin ignored the cold biting at his cheeks and pushed himself towards her. His body felt slow, half-asleep. "Evelyn stop!"

The door was rattling in its frame, shedding a curtain of icy flakes with every thump, but as Evelyn reached for its handle the shuddering stopped.

Too slow, Robin thought. *Too slow.*

The frozen air was almost silent and the theatre seemed to

hold its breath.

She gripped the door handle…

…and was yanked forward into the elevator room as the door pulled violently inwards. She stumbled into its black, formless interior and disappeared out of sight.

Robin leapt after her, launching himself towards the open doorway and the midnight beyond. The heavy red door swung closed. Robin crashed into it, his head and shoulders bouncing off hard timber. He landed in a heap, the frozen carpet brushing his back and burning his skin.

For a moment - or a few moments - he lay still, his head throbbing. Frost seemed to settle back down where he lay and his breath tingled ice on his lips.

"Evelyn," he murmured. The theatre was quiet. With a monumental effort, Robin clambered to his feet, trying to shake off his daze.

The cinema was white. Layer upon layer of frost had built up like snowdrifts. The thick fog was above the height of the seats now and would soon fill the theatre completely.

Robin pushed the Elevator Room door, almost falling onto it in his exhaustion. It swung open easily, revealing a well-lit plush red room with a sliver elevator door.

"Evelyn?" Robin whispered. He couldn't bring himself to step into the room, despite its warm appearance. "Evelyn?"

There was no answer. The empty room seemed to mock him and he backed away. Hot tears pierced into his chilled corneas and he quickly wiped them away before they could freeze. The mist was up to his shoulders.

Cursing himself for a coward, he turned away from the door. His body groaned as he forced it into a shuffling run along the back of the theatre, his footsteps loud on the icy carpet.

He was most of the way back to the camouflaged door when his knees barrelled into something on the floor. He stumbled and almost fell.

It was Diana. She was sitting on the frozen floor, barely visible in the thick white mist, her head hung between her knees. Frost had settled in her hair and on the tips of her ears.

After regaining his balance, Robin scooped Diana up in his arms, ignoring the crisp coldness of her skin. Grunting loudly, he hauled her to the camouflaged door and managed to yank it open with his fingertips.

The air in the booth was warm and dry as the door closed behind them, sealing out the freezing mist. Robin heaved a warm breath, feeling the painful chill in his lungs ease.

"Diana. Diana!" He set her down in front of the short ladder. She wavered but stood, her face damp, her lips shivering. "You've gotta climb. Quick!"

"Fucking righto," Diana muttered.

She climbed the ladder and waited at the top, arms wrapped around herself. Robin was right behind her. On heavy feet they ran though the kitchenette, dodging projectors and plates and boxes.

The horizontal window through to Cinema One was a solid block of opaque white.

17

The narrow bottom booth, as familiar to Robin as his own hands, was an island of calm. They stopped in the workshop, panting, looking at each other with wide eyes as the door settled shut.

"Where... where's Evelyn?" Diana gasped.

"I don't know." Robin squeezed his eyes shut in frustration. "We could have got out! We were right there. Why didn't you both just *follow* me?"

She stared in to space, her voice thin and hesitant. "There was crying. Someone asking... *begging*... for help."

A cold shiver drifted down Robin's spine. "Steven?"

Diana shook her head, pouting at the floor, whispering. "No. It wasn't Steven."

That's a good lookin woman you've got yourself, brother.

Another shiver. He rubbed at his arms, trying to soothe the goose bumps away.

"Where *is* she, Robin? Where did they go?"

Tell her everything.

"I... I don't know." He was staring at the sensor panel above the door; all of the lights were dark.

There was silence for a few moments.

Then Diana scowled. "It's *you*, isn't it?"

"What?" Robin was taken aback.

"*You're* doing all this." Fury was written all over her face. Her eyes gleamed. "It's *your* fucking cinema. The elevator, the fucking *air conditioner…*" She shoved at his chest.

His mouth hung open in disbelief. His throat worked, but at first nothing would come out. Finally he managed to croak. "You're kidding right?"

Diana advanced on him, her fear forgotten, her finger waving in his face. "*You* know how this place works. Am I some kind of a joke to you, Sam? *Where* are they?"

"I don't fucking know," Robin muttered, trying to sidestep her.

"You know *something!*" She grabbed his t-shirt with both hands, not letting him escape. "What ha…"

A loud squeal of feedback cut her off as light suddenly beamed into the booth through the projectionist's windows. It was coming from Cinemas Two and Three, a bright white light and a grinding electronic squeal that made Robin's eyes water and Diana's hands fly to her ears.

The light faded enough for them to look through the small horizontal window into Cinema Three. Robin felt the air leave his body when he saw what was on the screen.

"*Robin?*" Evelyn's tear-streaked face looked out at them.

It can't be.

She was somewhere dark and dirty, a crawlspace or even a wall cavity. Dusty wooden beams pressed her on both sides, trapping her arms. Her lower body was lost to darkness. There was a small cut on her forehead. "*Robin? Diana? I can't move. Diana?*"

Her voice echoed through the booth.

This can't be happening. Robin's head swam. Dimly, he felt

104

Diana press against him, her trembling fists gripping his t-shirt.

Light was flickering through the other horizontal window as well. Robin knew that if he looked into Cinema Two he would see the same thing; Evelyn's dirty, tear-streaked face, apparently trapped inside a narrow crawlspace or wall. *It's playing in all the theatres*, he thought, knowing it was true.

"This…" his throat was too dry so he swallowed and tried again. "The projectors aren't on."

"Robin?" Evelyn said again, her voice hitching. Her eyes were rolling from side to side, searching the darkness around her. One shoulder was wriggling as she tried to free her hands. *"Can you hear me?"*

"It can't be real," he murmured to Diana, his voice flat.

"Robin?" Evelyn gasped. Her shoulder stopped moving. *"Robin is that you?"*

"She couldn't possibly…"

"Robin? Can you hear me? Robin?"

Diana pushed away from him. "Evelyn! We can *see* you Evelyn!"

"Diana?" Evelyn sobbed in relief. *"Diana I'm stuck, I can't move."*

"Where are you?" Robin tried to keep the fear from his voice and failed. "Evelyn, where are you?"

"Robin?" She looked out into the darkness, wriggling her shoulders again. *"I don't know, you've gotta help me Robin I can't move!"*

"We can see you Ev, we're coming for you all right?" Tears were streaming down Diana's cheeks. "We're on our…"

Evelyn screamed and Robin lurched uselessly towards the window. Evelyn's shoulders were thrashing from side to side, her head smacking against the wall, her eyes bulging.

"Something's *touching* me! *Something's touching me!*"

Robin's blood turned to ice as Evelyn began to slide backwards into the dark. Her hysterical screams buzzed through his skull. He hit the window with his fist.

"No!"

"*Robin!*"

"Evelyn!" Diana sobbed, watching the screen in horror. "Evelyn *don't!*"

"*Robin!*" Something was dragging her down, pulling her through the dust and cobwebs and ancient timber, pulling her into the darkness below, screaming raw and terrible. "*No! Robin!*"

Shadows fell across her face as she was pulled down and out of view.

"*Robi...*"

The theatre shuddered with a loud, sickening, wet crunch.

"Evelyn!" Diana shrieked. "*Evelyn!*"

But the theatre was silent. The crawlspace was empty. She was gone.

Paralysed with shock, Robin stared at the screen as the last few drifting cobwebs and dirty grey timbers faded away. His heart thudded and his mind reeled.

There was a soft crying from his feet.

It wasn't real... the projectors weren't on... how could it be real... but he knew it was. He had been watching her. She had heard their voices.

Something brushed his calf. Diana had collapsed onto the floor, hiccupping and sobbing quietly.

Robin spared one more glance at the Cinema Three screen – it was completely dark now – then hauled Diana to her feet. She felt boneless and limp, but was thankfully light. He set her on her feet and waited for her to steady. She wouldn't look at him.

"She's gone, isn't she." Her voice was dull. "They're both gone."

No. She can't be.

The sensor panel above the door was blind. No movement, anywhere in the building.

"They're both *dead.*"

"No," Robin hissed. "You saw her, we both *saw* her. She's here somewhere."

Suddenly she shoved him, hard and violent.

"*Bullshit!* Bullshit, Samuel!" Her face was twisted in fury. "You told me you would fucking *leave* her. How could you… how could she…?"

"I'm not gonna leave her." *Tell her everything.* "We need to look for them."

She scowled. "I need to get the *fuck* out of here and that's what I'm gonna do."

"But if we can…"

"*Robin!*" She screamed in his face. "Get me *the fuck* out of here!"

He turned his back to her, peering back into Cinema Three. It was still.

"There are two exits down there, one in each cinema. I'll come downstairs with you, then you can take your pick."

"Why not just go out the front door?" she demanded, crossing her arms.

"You do what you want." He glowered as he pushed past her. "I'm going to find Evelyn. Let's go." He held the door open.

She hesitated, not meeting his eyes, then reached out and took something from the workshop bench.

A Stanley knife, Robin thought. *For all the good that will do.* He turned and walked out.

After a moment, she followed.

18

They were halfway down the stairs when the lights went out.

Diana gave a little shriek that bounced off the concrete walls and tingled Robin's fraying nerves. The darkness was absolute in the stairwell, with nowhere for light to leak in. Robin clutched at his breast pocket, relieved to find his trusty Maglite in its usual place.

"Robin?" Diana's voice shook, just behind him.

He took the torch from his breast pocket and flicked it on. Its bright light split the darkness like a laser. Diana clutched at him and he could feel her shaking in the few moments before she let him go. Their breathing was loud. Nothing moved.

"Come on," Robin said, his throat hoarse.

They followed the torchlight down to the foyer door. Diana waited while Robin slowly pushed it ajar and peered through the crack.

It wasn't as dark in the foyer. Street lights poured in through the mezzanine's glass doors and bounced off all the polished surfaces. It looked much the same as it always did with the lights off; oddly placid but full of anticipation, like an uninflated balloon.

Or a sleeping dragon, Robin thought, disquieted.

Jim Carrey was beaming up at the ceiling where posters dangled, motionless, the victims of a silent lynching. The Candy Bar seemed cold and unwelcoming, its rows of lollies and chocolate bars robbed of colour by the dim light. David's office door was firmly closed.

"Okay, come on" Robin whispered.

They crept through the foyer, tiptoeing past Jim's enormous face. Robin's torchlight played across the floor, the walls, the ceiling. Diana's eyes were wide as she tried to look everywhere at once.

"Are those doors unlocked?" She whispered, nodding at the front entrance.

"They're always unlocked from the inside," Robin told her. "You just push on the bar in the middle and they'll open, but..."

"But what?"

"What about Evelyn? And Steven?"

"I'm getting out of here," she said, her voice louder. She marched across the foyer, away from his torchlight and towards the stairs. "And I'm calling the police. This is insane."

"Wait, Diana!"

She ignored him so he followed her, jogging to catch up and reaching her at the mezzanine stairs. She wouldn't look at him.

"Diana, the police won't believe any..."

"Shit!" She stopped walking and her eyes were wide. "Look!"

He looked. The streetlight coming in through the glass doors was fading, dimming. The buildings across the road were harder to see and even the footpath just outside was growing dark, as though Brisbane Street itself was fading away.

No, realised Robin. *It's smoke.*

The street wasn't disappearing – a thick black haze was filling the mezzanine, obscuring the view of the outside world and cutting off the light. It darkened and shifted, easing into curls of smoke. He pointed the beam of his Maglite into it. Clouds of the darkest greys roiled in the beam, thick and menacing, pulsing as though driven by a chimney - or a roaring inferno. It grew thicker by the second, filling the mezzanine until Brisbane Street was lost to sight.

There were shapes moving in the smoke, figures made of shifting black strands, shades of darker darkness. Robin's throat tasted of bitter ash, of burning wool and timber and meat.

"Diana," he coughed, waving the torch back and forth across the mezzanine, reaching for her with his free hand.

She was backing down the stairs, away from the smoke, but it rolled down the stairs with an impossible churning weight, spreading and blooming out from itself.

Something reached out of the black cloud, reaching for Diana, its fingers trailed by decaying tendrils of smoke. The blurred, indistinct hand wrapped around Diana's wrist and tried to drag her away,

"*Robin!*" Her high-pierced cry shook him. "*Help me!*"

"Diana!" Robin's fingers wrapped around her other elbow. The Maglite's beam swung chaotically as he tried to pull her away. When the torchlight fell across the shade's hand it disappeared from sight, but its strength didn't waiver and the hand reappeared as the torchlight rolled.

Robin's feet were slipping from under him "No!" He heaved at Diana with all of his weight and, for a wonder, the shade slipped from her arm and she was free. She stumbled down the steps after Robin, somehow pushing him to keep him on his feet.

They ran. The smoke buffeted itself and then surged, alive,

following them.

"This way!"

He led her through the Cinema Three doors, away from the simmering smoke and the furious shades and Jim Carrey's good-natured grin.

19

The old, well-oiled hinges of the Cinema Three doors seemed to sigh as they swung closed. Robin led Diana into the silent, pitch black theatre. Thick shadows seemed to embrace them. *Even the aisle lights are off.*

The Maglite was cool and heavy in his hand, its light piercing into the cavernous theatre. There was only one speck of light in all that gloom – the dim green *Exit* sign. Next to the screen, at the end of a dark aisle that seemed to stretch longer and longer into the dark...

He stumbled into Diana and she clutched at him in reflex. Even in the near dark he could see her trembling.

"Diana?" He kept his voice low.

She fumbled for his arm and pulled him close. "Why's it so *dark?*"

"Come on."

He pulled her towards the aisle then stopped short, his stomach sinking.

A burned, misshapen figure stood in the aisle, blocking the way. Its body was disfigured and burned, its gown and head-scarf scorched and threadbare, flecked with gold. Furious eyes glared from the charred ruin of its face, unflinching in the stark torchlight.

Robin tried to cry out, but fear froze the word in his throat.

"Robin?" Diana's fingers dug into his shoulder.

"You." Its voice was harsh and dry, ashes breaking from charcoal.

"Yes." His voice shook. He licked his lips.

"Let's *go!*" Diana pulled at him.

"You came back." The grit in its words made Robin want to shriek. *"For me? Or. For her."* It twisted the last word, choked on it.

"Get out of my way," he demanded through clenched teeth, drawing on some unknown stubbornness. *"Move."* He didn't want to look at it. It *hurt* to look at it.

"Robin," whimpered Diana. "There's nobody there."

"She is mine," the thing hissed, abruptly spinning away from him into the darkness. Fury dripped from its words. *"Start the show!"*

"Robin," Diana cried, shaking him.

"Start the show!"

"Run! *Run!*" Robin's feet took off of their own volition and he sprinted down the barely-visible aisle towards the Exit sign. Diana's footsteps were right behind him. She was whimpering, hyperventilating.

A furious, bone-grinding scream rattled the sea of red seats.

Robin darted to the left of the screen and hit the exit door at full steam. Relief flooded his body as light spilled into the theatre through the open door; the lights in the exit room, running on their own UPS circuit, were still on.

Something hit him in the back and pushed him into the room. Diana. As Robin pulled the door closed he stared in wonder at the theatre they had just run through. Liquid darkness was flowing from beneath the seats, bubbling across the floor towards him, a shadow within a shadow, malicious and intent.

"The exit," he yelled, shutting the door against the oozing tide. "Go!"

Diana was up the steps in a flash but as she reached the door she stopped in her tracks.

Before Robin could urge her on, she threw back her head and screamed, a scream thick with hysteria. Robin rushed to her then had to stifle his own shocked yelp.

There was a body on the floor. Prone, face down. Blocking the exit.

"Is it him? Is it him?" Diana was panting. "Is it Steven?"

Robin sank to his knees, shaking his head. He knew it wasn't Steven even before he gently turned the body over.

Oh man. Buckley.

He had never made it out of the building. Robin's gut churned as he took in his old friend's wet clothes and hair, his rolled up shirtsleeves, his wrinkled fingers, his blue lips. The water pooling in his eyes, never to be blinked away.

"What happened to him?" Diana asked. Her hands were balled into shaking fists.

"Look at him," Robin said. Buckley's big hands were pale and bloated, as white as a fish's belly. "I think he drowned."

"Drowned? In here?" She shook her head. "How is that possible?"

There was click and a hiss above them as the emergency sprinkler system switched on.

Diana gaped at Robin in horror as icy water rained down on them. The sprinklers gushed, flooding the carpeted floor in seconds.

She shoved past him and stepped over Buckley's body, throwing herself at the exit door, rattling and thumping.

"It won't open!" she screamed.

Robin helped her push at the door to no avail. Water thundered into the room, falling from the sprinklers in a constant stream. His ankles spiked with cold and Robin swore; the trapped water was already above his ankles and rising.

Rising fast.

"Help! Help us!" Diana was banging on the exit door with the flat of her hand. "We can't get out!"

Coldness enveloped Robin's knees as the dark water rose higher and faster. Robin saw with horror that Buckley's body had lifted off the floor, floating and bobbing like a paper boat. He tried to avoid touching it as he sploshed past to try the door back into the theatre. Diana abandoned the exit to come and help him.

"Push!" Robin shouted over the noise of falling water. "Push it!"

They pushed with everything they had, again and again. Nothing. The door might well have been set in stone. The water tickled their waists.

"Why won't it open?" Diana cried, hysteria livid in her voice. Buckley's body floated towards her and her sobs became faster and higher pitched until Robin reached out and pushed it away. It bobbed as water streamed onto it from the sprinklers above.

"Give me the knife!"

Diana hesitated, fear and distrust clear in her eyes. The freezing water was well above her breasts now.

"Diana *come on!*"

She passed it to him. Moving quickly, Robin pulled out the blade and eased it into the crack above the door, slicing along the gap, dragging it this way and that, looking for purchase, finding none.

"These fucking doors aren't watertight," Robin growled in helpless rage. "You can't even *lock* them! We're not fucking *drowning* in here!"

But the water brushing both the top of his shoulders and Buckley's floating corpse seemed to disagree.

Diana's sobs were stilted hiccups now, her breath labouring.

She's treading water, Robin realised. He reached out and propped her up, standing on his toes to keep their heads above the freezing water. He could see the terror in her darting eyes, her pleading tears. He tried to think of something to say. *Should have eaten your veggies, Diana.*

Abruptly the lights flicked off. Diana screamed.

The tiny room, almost completely submerged in near-freezing water, was now in total darkness.

It got us. It got us. We're going to die in here.

Diana was sobbing. "Robin? Robin?"

Robin couldn't see, but he felt her hands clutching at him in the water. Coldness splashed against his cheeks and he tried to keep her propped up, tried not to think about Buckley's body floating next to them...

And then his face was underwater.

Panic made his legs kick. He swam up off the floor, breaking the surface, but he couldn't hold Diana up as well. She slipped below the surface with a swallowed yelp.

Robin reached up instinctively, the blade still in his fist. He could feel the air in the bare hand span between the water's surface and the ceiling, but he couldn't get his face up to it and the gap was closing. Everything swirled in the dark. A thrashing foot caught his thigh.

Air. Air. Need air.

With more reflex than purpose, Robin shoved the Stanley

knife into the carpeted ceiling above. It cracked and gave way, just a little.

Diana was scrabbling at his shoulders, her nails biting into his neck, but he couldn't hear her anymore. His ears were full of water.

With a last, desperate jab he pushed the knife at the ceiling... and it broke through.

Blessed light pierced the black water.

Working mindlessly, his lungs burning, Robin jabbed at the ceiling again and again, using the knife's heavy handle to break the plaster, twisting the blade to cut the carpet away. In a few moments, the hole was bigger than his fist, so he pushed both hands into it and *pulled* as hard as he could.

Plaster crumbled away like cardboard. Light washed over him. He tore at the edges, ripping away more and more plaster until there was enough of a hole to stick his head through.

Sweet, sweet oxygen filled his lungs. He blinked away the light and had time to register another set of hands pulling the plaster away before he took a deep breath and pushed himself back underwater.

He found Diana's kicking legs and wrapped his arms around them, pushing her up towards the ceiling, towards the light. She wriggled upwards, abruptly took her own weight... and was gone.

Robin poked his up head through the hole again. Diana was on her knees next to the hole, gulping air, her heaves whistling, her eyes frantic.

Upon seeing him, she seized his waving arm and leaned back, pulling with all her weight. Robin kicked his legs in the dark water. In a few moments he was out as well, rolling onto his back, gasping. Cold water ran from his hair and clothes, making quick rivulets on the impossibly dusty carpet.

They laid where they were for a moment, catching their breath. The water's surface settled an inch or two below the ripped plaster and frayed carpet edging. Everything was still.

Where the fuck are we? Robin propped himself up on his elbows.

They were in a long, narrow hallway with a high roof. Deep red walls were lined with exposed wooden pillars and huge, indistinct paintings in gaudy ornate frames. The carpet may have been red once, but dust and age had faded it.

The air tasted ancient. It was too dark to see the end of the hallway. It might have gone on forever.

Diana was sobbing softly. Robin reached out and she seized his hand and sat up next to him, trying to control her breathing. She let go after a moment though and climbed to her feet, her body shuddering with sobs, her damp skin pallid. Water dripped from her clothes, pooling around her feet as she regarded Robin miserably.

"I want to go home," she whimpered.

There was a sudden splash behind her and a wet, white hand thrust out of the hole in the floor. With vicious speed, it latched around Diana's ankle in an iron grip and violently yanked her back with brutal, impossible strength.

Diana didn't have time to scream, or to catch herself. She hit the floor face first. Robin saw her head bounce, heard the sickening thud. His mind reeled. Horror froze him to the spot.

"Diana…"

The dripping fish-white arm, powerful and implacable, pulled her into the hole in the floor. She was sliding across the dusty carpet, moaning weakly, trying to struggle.

Dropping to his knees, Robin lunged for her… but he was

too late.

She slid back into the icy water, back into the dark.

And then she was gone.

Buckley, Robin thought, numb.

The water rippled for a few moments and was still.

20

S tale dust permeated the dim hallway. It drifted languorously around him. There was only enough light to see a few metres ahead and the corridor seemed to go on forever.

Two people. Dead. In my *cinema. Three if I count Steven.* Robin shook as he crept through the dimness. *Four if I count Evelyn.*

His hands were a mess of dust and tears. His shoes squelched loudly with each step, the dust beneath them mixing in to a thin grey paste. The hole in the floor was lost to the darkness behind him.

You're the only one who knows how this place works.

Abruptly his head was spinning and he stopped, bent at the waist, eyes squeezed closed, waiting for the dizziness to pass.

Turns out I don't know shit.

Back down the hallway there was a gentle splash, dripping, and several dull thuds.

Robin froze.

Something else came out of the water. Someone else is here.

A wave of exhausted fear washed over him. His legs felt weak, like they might suddenly drop him onto the dusty floor.

"Diana?" There was a dry croak in his throat.

Water was dripping off... someone. He could hear it spattering on the carpet. It was too dark to see that far down the hall.

"Diana?" He swallowed. "Buckley?"

There was a footstep, a squelch. Then another. It was coming.

Gasping, Robin turned and willed his legs to move. He ran, the carpet sickly soft beneath his feet. Wet, smacking thuds followed.

The hallway stretched ahead in the dark. *A dead end,* Robin thought bleakly. *It'll be a dead end.*

But it wasn't. A few more steps and the hallway became a wooden staircase built from dark hardwood.

Where am I? Above the foyer? Behind the booth? It didn't matter. He tried to shrug off the disorientation. The stairs beneath his feet didn't creak, solid despite their obvious age and lack of use.

He glanced back over his shoulder. A shadow in the shadows, drawing closer. Fighting off panic, he pushed harder - and his shoes, slick with wet muddy dust, slipped on the hard timber.

His feet went from under him and he fell, heavily, onto the unforgiving timber stairs. Wooden edges smacked into his bicep, his hip and his thigh. He managed to turn his head to save his jaw from crashing into the polished timber, but his left knee twisted with a nasty grinding sound of bone against bone and he grunted in pain.

Oh shit that hurt. That fuckin hurt. He had to keep moving. He crawled up the stairs, trying to find purchase with his feet, his left leg numb and refusing to take orders.

The footsteps were drawing closer and closer now.

Don't look.

The door at the top of the stairs was plain, heavy timber. Robin laid a hand on it, the hair on the back of his neck bristling.

The old-fashioned iron handle, high above his head, could have been a mile away.

A wet, flopping sound, a timber squish. Another. It was climbing the stairs.

Robin reached for the door handle, straining, holding his breath. His fingertips brushed it.

A soft drip dripping and another wet thud. The smell of damp was cloying in the small space.

Don't look!

Robin leaned into the wooden door, pulling himself up. His body was weak, disconnected, a million miles away, but his hand found the door handle and he used it to heave himself upright.

Another squishing step. Just behind him. Almost within reach.

He looked.

An indistinct figure was reaching for him, water dripping from grey limbs. A flash of pale skin; a hand, unfamiliar, bloated and damp. The stink of damp dust filled Robin's lungs.

Cold panic swept through him and he shoved mindlessly backwards, scrabbling at the iron handle... until the dry timber door suddenly opened and he fell back into warm lamplight, crashing and rolling onto a plush claret carpet.

The door slammed closed behind him, heavy and irrevocable.

21

It *reeked* in here, wherever *here* was. Robin pushed himself up from the carpet and gagged at the stink filling his nostrils. His left knee was throbbing with bright awkward pain and his entire body shivered uncontrollably, but he managed to get to his feet and look around.

A *theatrette,* Robin wondered. It's *an old theatrette. The cinema must have been built around it.*

Heavy red curtains hung from low walls to bunch up artfully on the carpet. Old fashioned lamps protruded from between the curtains, seeming to make more shadow than light. At one end of the room was a polished wooden bar lined with dusty glasses and bottles. At the other end was a small, darkened performer's stage with more thick velvet hanging to either side. A dozen or so black leather chairs were scattered through the room, facing the stage. Most of the seats were empty. Some were not.

Robin's stomach lurched and his chest seemed to collapse into a tight, airless knot. Any strength he might have possessed, to run or move or even scream, deserted him.

The dozen or so people slouching motionless in the dark might have been waiting for a show to start, except for the lifeless glass of their eyes, the sunken darkness of their cheeks.

An audience of the dead.

Bodies. So many bodies. All waiting for the show.

They were slumped in their chairs or sprawled awkwardly across the carpet, almost a dozen bodies in various states of decay. Some were skeletal, their skin stretched and dried and wrapped in raggedy suits tinted by decades of dust. One still had a wolfish slick of brittle black hair clinging to his disintegrating skull. But the others...

You're the only one who knows how this place works.

Steven sat upright in the one of the black chairs. His chin dangled loosely onto his chest, as though he had fallen asleep watching TV, except that his eyes were wide open and unseeing. His right arm had been torn off and his shoulder ended in a bloody, ragged stump. There was blood on his crotch, as well as scratches and grazes on his cheeks and forehead. However he had died, it hadn't come easy.

There was another body he recognised. Old mate was slumped back in his seat, his mouth hanging wide open to reveal the white flesh of his mouth and an arc of yellowed teeth. His skin had shrivelled and torn in more than a few places and what was left clung to his bones. He was still wearing the neat grey suit that Robin had found him in just a few weeks ago, the scarlet necktie snug around the rotting gristle of his throat.

Dead. Dead and gone.

On the floor just behind him was a woman's body. Her face was oddly twisted to stare unblinking at the ceiling. Her skin was soft and pallid, her hair dank and wet against the collar of her filthy yellow blou...

A light clunked on over the stage.

Robin spun, adrenaline pouring down his spine.

Evelyn.

It *was* her. Relief washed through him, but only momentarily. She was laying very still. *Too* still.

She was slumped across the small stage, face down, her hair loose, her clothes mostly gone. Her body was a rainbow of yellows and purples, lashed with deep scarlet, filthy with grime and scale, raw and mottled and stinging. Robin's stomach roiled at the sight and bile gurgled in his chest.

He took a step towards her... and froze.

The dead were watching him. Though Robin hadn't seen them move, their faces had all turned towards him and now they stared, some with the empty sockets of dusty skulls, some with eyes bright and clear and knowing amongst the slack ruins of their faces. Steven's body was sitting up straight in its chair, its unblinking eyes fixed on Robin. A young man with blue lips and a filthy khaki jacket scowled across the room. Even the dried, dusty corpses on the carpet had twisted their papery necks to gape at him.

Robin took a step back, away from those glaring dead eyes. The bright stage light made the rest of the room dim. The heavy red curtains seemed closer, as if the room was shrinking.

"Samuel?" Her voice was soft, disbelieving.

Evelyn was sitting upright on the stage. A patchy white slip hung loosely from her shoulders and clung to her midriff. A heavy chain snaked away from the iron manacle enclosing her ankle. The other end was bolted to an anchor point at the back of the stage. There were more points spread along the back wall. On the front of the stage, well out of her reach, a small key hung from a nail.

"Samuel?"

Robin's heart pounded as he turned to her. "I came back for you." It didn't sound like his voice. They didn't feel like his words.

"Help me." Barely above a whisper. "Please. Take me away from here." She followed his gaze to the steel manacle around her ankle and started to cry.

"Why did you come, Sugarplum?" He heard himself say. "Why would you come to this place?"

Evelyn sobbed. "They won't let me leave. She... told me..."

"She's a *liar*," he growled, furious.

"She told me that you... you... *Samuel!*"

A cold hand seized Robin's throat, strong as a vice. Panic and terror electrified him and he reached up to pull the dead hand away but a sudden, *excruciating* pain exploded in his side.

He yelped, a thin and hopeless yelp choked out of him by the cold hand wringing his neck.

Another chilly, damp hand was pushing into him, just below the ribcage. It was wrapped around the hilt of a Stanley knife, pushing the thin blade deep into Robin's gut. Abruptly it was yanked away, slicing through soft flesh as it exited his body.

Pain exploded through Robin's body. Blood poured from his side. His knees buckled.

"*Sam!*" Evelyn shrieked and lunged against her chain. "*Sam! NO!*"

The room swam in and out of focus. Spinning red velvet threatened to smother him. He stumbled back one step, then another, then got tangled in his feet and fell onto his back next to the bar. The impact made him scream and he clutched at the leaking hole in his side.

Diana was standing over him. Diana had stabbed him.

Not Diana. Diana is dead. They're all dead. Whatever had stabbed him, it *wasn't* the drunkenly vivacious girl he had met only a few hours earlier.

Straining against the agony in his torso, Robin could see it looking down at him, the dripping blade still in its hand. As he watched, it reached down to pick up a gold cloche hat from the carpet and fix it upon its dusty damp hair. Apparently satisfied, it turned away from him.

"No, no, no Samuel please!" Evelyn was sobbing, reaching for him, pulling against the iron manacle. *"Sam! Sam!"*

I've gotta get up. Robin tried to bite down on his cries, but he was so weak. *Broken. I'm broken.*

He laid back, trying to breathe properly, trying to stem the bleeding with his hand, trying to focus on Evelyn's weeping, trying to ward off the fog that was creeping into his brain.

The red velvet curtains glowed and swayed. There was blood in his mouth. His body was loose, disconnected, boneless. The soft carpet was warm where his skin was sinking into it, like the carpet of his parent's farmhouse all those years ago when it had been summer and he was a dozing, sleepy boy.

Just close your eyes. Close your eyes. Get your strength back, just for a tick. Warmth oozed between his fingers.

"Sam... *Sam?"* Evelyn's terrified voice broke through his haze. "Sam *help me!"*

He heard the cold clink of steel and the soft rustle of movement. Gritting his teeth, he opened his eyes and lifted his head.

The other bodies were moving now. They shifted in their seats, heads lolling on shrivelled necks. Some were climbing to their feet and shuffling purposefully towards the stage. Diana was settling into a chair, apparently to watch.

"No! No more!" Evelyn's shrieks were oddly dampened in the muffled room. *"Sam. Please,* Sam."

Robin tried to sit up, but his side burned and moving was

white agony.

"*No*. Get *away!*"

The terror and fury in her voice rocked him. He pushed back with his feet, his knee grinding painfully, until he was sitting upright against the timber bar. He tried to catch his breath.

Whimpering, Evelyn knelt in the centre of the stage, face down. She was shaking, taking deep breaths, gulping at the air...then all at once she seemed to settle. For a moment she was still... then she lifted her head.

To Robin's horror, she was smiling. It was a terrible smile, a curling grimace that showed her teeth but didn't touch her eyes. Her shoulders shook and tears ran down her cheeks, but she was smiling.

Two dead men were climbing on to the stage.

One was a shambling stick-thin mess of dusty suit and crumbling skin, wisps of gossamer hair drifting about its papery temples. Its livid eyes, intent and almost human, were fixed on Evelyn's body.

The other was Steven. Expressionless, mouth hanging open, eyes bulging, suit a bloody mess below his missing arm.

Kneeling between them, Evelyn closed her eyes, smiling her awful smile.

Robin hauled himself to his feet. It was agony. He leaned on the timber, his breath hitching, his hand bumping the small pyramid of old-fashioned whisky glasses that sat on the bar. Half a dozen bottles sat next to them, gleaming with silver, tawny, and aqua green spirits.

Evelyn leaned forward onto her hands as Steven reached down with his remaining hand, gently laying it across the small of her back. She raised her smiling face, squeezed her eyes shut and arched her spine obediently.

The old corpse slowly sunk to its knees beside her. Robin saw the grey tongue slither over its teeth, the mottled, mouldy fingers stretching, itching to touch her.

"No!" Robin rasped. *"Don't!"*

Steven's dead fingers stroked along Evelyn's skin, pulling at her slip. The sheer material drifted higher up the backs of her thighs and he leaned in to...

A heavy glass bottle smashed in to Steven's face. He swayed, unbalanced, and fell onto his back in a rain of vodka and broken glass. Something white and red dropped from his pocket - the *Ruby Club* matchbook flipped open as it skittered across the stage, revealing a complete set of unused matches.

The next bottle that Robin threw smashed uselessly into the back of the stage, but his third flew straight and fast and thumped into the old corpse's decrepit torso, knocking it backwards. Robin moved closer, his twisted knee forgotten, the hole in his side forgotten, another heavy glass bottle ready in his hand.

His next throw took the old corpse in the temple. The bottle didn't break, but *something* did, broke with a crunch and a thud. The body fell into a heap on the stage.

A sour sweet reek of old alcohol eased through the theatrette. Robin took another bottle from the bar – the second last one. Hefting its weight in his hand, he turned to throw it at the stage... but Diana was there, standing almost toe to toe with him, the Stanley knife bright in her hand.

Robin dropped the bottle with a startled gasp and Diana's arm shot out and seized his throat. Freezing cold fingers pushed painfully into his skin. Air squeezed out of him. She lifted him off the carpet and he dangled from her hand like a ragdoll. Brightness flared in his vision, silver sparks and yellow flames, and he kicked and swung to no avail.

Diana's corpse held him by the throat, pushing him against the bar, her face just inches away from his own.

Dead eyes examined him. She whispered. "I would have given you *anything*, Sam."

For a horrifying moment, Robin thought she would kiss him. *Don't. Don't. I'll lose my mind.*

But the corpse didn't kiss him. Instead she swung the knife, a flashing silver arc plunging towards his heart.

The blade struck his chest... and deflected away with a loud *ping.* The thin razor point was no match for the heavy steel of his Maglite torch.

Bright, scarlet pain scored across his ribs as the knife sliced his skin open instead of plunging into his chest. Diana was thrown off balance as her weight followed the blade's interrupted path. Her grip on his throat loosened.

Moving instinctively, sucking at the smoky air, Robin seized the last bottle from the bar - *Van Diemen Malt* – and swung it in a sweeping backhand with all the strength he could muster.

The bottle caught her under the jaw and smashed to pieces. Her head rocked back, but the hand on Robin's throat didn't let go. Black spots were spreading across his vision, pushing against the flickering yellow flames.

With the last of his strength, Robin raised the bottle's jagged neck and brought it plunging down into the dead thing's face. She shuddered, her hand trembling. Robin yanked the bottle neck out of her ruined face and swept it down again and again... and on the fourth blow Diana's hand went limp.

He fell out of her grip and collapsed to the floor coughing and gasping.

The corpse, no longer recognisable as the girl it had been, fell on the carpet next to him, the Stanley knife still in her hand. Robin whimpered and tried to roll away, but he pushed into something else on the carpet.

Another body was laying on the floor next to him, in a prone position almost identical to his own. It was long-decayed, given to dry dust, but its cotton tunic was still a mess of dried black blood. The old bloodstains spread out from both a hole near the ribs and a short dagger that still protruded from its chest.

Samuel, thought Robin, groggy. *You* did *come back*.

The stage was on fire. Thick smoke rolled along the ceiling, trapped in the small theatrette. A few of the corpses were still moving – the woman in yellow was crawling along the floor towards the door – but most sat motionless in their chairs, staring at Evelyn.

She was staring at *him*. Her face was a portrait of disbelief.

"Evelyn." Robin took a few careful steps towards the stage. The painful glow in his side was flaring, the strip across his chest oozing blood into his work shirt.

Her eyes never left him as he limped to the stage. The curtains behind her were swinging, blazing sheets that framed her against a wall of fire.

Robin took the key off the nail, leaning on the stage, sighing as some of the pressure was taken off his side. His breath was ragged and painful. "Evelyn, come on."

Dazed, she lifted her foot towards him. He grabbed it and worked the key into the rusted manacle around her ankle.

Cold, her foot is so cold.

After some convincing, the key turned. The irons clanked to the stage. Flames climbed the velvet curtains on all sides, teasing them with black smoke before engulfing them. The roof dripped fire.

21

Evelyn lowered her foot, staring at him. "You're not Samuel."

A chill ran down his spine. "No."

The smell of ancient whisky blended headily into the smoke drifting over them, filling Robin's aching lungs with an acrid stink. *It's this place. I've gotta get her out of this place.*

"Come on." He held a hand out to her, his eyes darting amongst the shifting shadows caused by the rising flames. "Evelyn *come on!*"

She stared at his hand, then at his face, hesitating. After an endless moment she reached out and he helped her off the burning stage. Neither Steven nor the old corpse moved.

The only door out of the theatrette was on fire. Slumped against it was the woman in yellow, her dead hands clasped around the handle, her bulk collapsed on to the smouldering wood.

I can't move her, Robin thought. His strength was ebbing. Flames were leaping to life all around them. *We've gotta get out of here.*

In desperation he lifted a foot and drove it into the woman's back. She shoved into burning door and the door broke away from its frame, splintering into smoke and charcoal.

Robin stared at the stairs and hallway beyond the door. It was burning, all of it, a roiling, lethal inferno. Awash with high flames, the timber stairs were impossible to pass. Flames crawled across the red walls and black smoke roared back into the theatrette.

It was hard to breathe. Hot ash swirled through the air, singeing his face. He couldn't see the door, couldn't see three feet in front of him, but he could feel Evelyn's cold hand still tight in his own.

The smoke was thick and getting thicker, swelling with every second… and it was moving. It drifted towards the bar, to the wall *behind* the bar. Something underneath the shelves seemed to be drawing the smoke, breathing it in.

There! The smoke was streaming towards a small cellar door, nestled just out of sight behind the bar. As Robin watched, the smoke was pulled in to the cracks around the door.

"Come on!" His voiced rasped, dry, as he followed the twirling smoke behind the bar. The roof dripped fire and ember. Heat and smoke washed over him. He pulled Evelyn to the small door and wrenched it open.

Flames surged as fresh air poured into the theatrette, an enormous gush of heat and light that knocked Evelyn off her feet. A blast of heat rushed over them, embers stinging wherever they landed. The theatrette roared, a squirming fireball.

He hauled Evelyn off the floor.

"Evelyn! *Evelyn!*" He shook her to no avail. "Evelyn!"

Her eyes were closed, her body unresponsive. *We've* gotta *get out of here now!*

Smoke whirled around him, upwards and away through the cellar door. *Steps, there are steps.* He could just make out the bottom two slabs of rough-hewn concrete. Falling to his knees, Robin crawled through the opening into a dark passageway.

Where the fuck will this take us? He couldn't even guess anymore. He guided Evelyn's unconscious body through the doorway and onto the bottom step then reached back for the door, trying to pull it shut. Each breath burned in his lungs. When his hand found the thin timber door he yanked it shut, plunging them into near darkness.

The smoke twisted past, streaming towards a dim light above. The stairs were narrow and steep. Embers were already settling on the floor and sticking to the walls. Soon, this passage would be on fire too.

Coughing and wheezing, Robin pulled Evelyn up the stairs, his body an orchestra of pain. The concrete on all sides grew hotter and hotter by the moment and the air was searing and thin his throat, but adrenaline drove him on. Soon they reached another small landing and another cellar door.

Holding his breath, Robin unlatched the door and it swung inwards. *Don't be a brick wall, don't be a brick wall...*

It didn't open to a brick wall. It opened to a wall of paper. The door to the theatrette had been hidden behind a sheet of paper. Old, thick fibrous paper, almost like...

You've gotta be fucking kidding.

He pushed the paper with an unsteady hand and it tore easily, splitting with the barest resistance. He ripped it out of the way and squeezed through the small doorway into the light, pulling Evelyn along with him... and breathed the most delicious air he had ever known deeply into his lungs.

22

They were in the Bunker. His home.

All this time, his little bedsit had contained a hidden door. *To a private fucking dungeon, no less.* Even with the smoke pouring out of the open cellar door, he took a moment to wonder.

The poster they had emerged through, *Gilda,* had mostly come off the wall when he pushed his way through it. But Rita Heyworth was still there, smiling saucily at both his stupidity and her own tenacious mystery.

Acrid smoke stung his nostrils again. He pulled the cellar door shut, for all the good *that* would do. The whole building would be alight soon, if it wasn't already.

"Evelyn, wake up! Ev! *Ev!*" He shook her shoulders, but her eyes didn't flicker. "Goddamn it, Ev, wake *up.*"

She wasn't waking up. Straining, he lifted her off the floor and hauled her through the Bunker in his arms. *We're done with this joint. Sorry Uncle David.* Rita Heyworth watched them go.

Carrying her down the stairs wasn't easy. His side tricked blood and most of his torso throbbed to a dull beat. His knee might buckle beneath him on any step. He shifted her awkwardly, navigated the handrail and the concrete steps and paused on each landing to catch his breath, drawing in the crisp cool of the concrete stairwell air. Sweat dripped down his back, or maybe it was more blood.

Finally he kicked open the door of the Candy Bar storeroom and they emerged into the cool bottom foyer. Robin carefully laid Evelyn down on one of the big ottomans, then stepped over to the Candy Bar.

Reaching across the counter, he found the stack of large cardboard drinking cups and sat two of them on the soda machine's plastic drip tray. The water that came out was cool and fresh and hit his parched throat like mana from heaven.

He had half-filled the enormous cups when he heard an unfamiliar electrical squelch. *The fire.*

Evelyn was still unconscious. Moving as quickly as he could, Robin jogged over to the Cinema Three doors and threw them open, wincing against the smoke and ashes...

But there was no smoke, no ashes. No heat. No sign of the fire at all. The theatre looked much the same as it always did. He reached up and laid a gentle hand on the carpeted wall. *That long hallway* has *to be behind this wall.* There was no way the fire had been about to stop and nowhere else it could have...

That electric squelch again, louder this time. It wasn't the fire, or even a crackle in one of the huge speakers that were built into the walls of the theatre. It was little more than an electronic chirp, a distant alarm perhaps.

Robin's strength had returned enough for him to try and lift her off the ottoman. While there was no sign of it down here, the fire still had to be burning somewhere. *One more set of stairs and we're out.* He scooped her up, awkwardly favouring his left side, and carried her to the mezzanine stairs.

Halfway up, she stirred in his arms.

Oh thank Christ. He knelt on the steps and lay her gently

down on the mezzanine's carpet. She rolled onto her back and stretched her grimy arms and bruised legs. Her eyes fluttered open. For a few moments she simply stared at her hands, stunned, then she looked around the mezzanine in wonder.

"Evelyn," Robin said, touching her face. "Evvie, it's okay. We're back. You're back. It's gonna be okay, Ev."

She jerked her head towards him, looked him up and down. "You're not Samuel."

All of the air squeezed out of his chest. *No*, he thought. *No, no, no.*

Panic bloomed. Wave after wave of cold adrenaline coursed through him, but when he spoke he was numb. Distant.

"Samuel's gone," he said. "He came back for you and they killed him."

She didn't say anything for a few moments, then lowered her head. "I saw. She lied to me. I was bait, it was *him* she wanted."

Robin shivered. Some part of his mind was screaming, yammering at him to get away, but he was frozen to the spot. "I'm sorry."

"I burned them. I burned it all." She turned away from him. What she saw out of the glass entry doors made her she gasp. There was wonder in her voice. "That's sunlight."

"Yeah," he frowned. *Don't let her leave.* Don't *let her leave.* "Yeah, it's morning."

She stood up. He scrambled to his feet as well as he could, limping along after her as she glided towards the front doors.

If she leaves now, she'll never be Evelyn again. He didn't know why he was so sure of it, but he was.

"Wait, Ev, I don't think…"

"I've been trying to get away from here for a long, long time," she gazed through the glass, ignoring him.

Stop her Robin!

Before he could move, Evelyn leaned into the glass door, pushing into the silver bar that should have opened it. But the door didn't open. It wouldn't move. She shoved as it again, but it just rattled in the frame.

"Evelyn, wait."

She tried the next door but it wouldn't open either. She growled in frustration and abruptly the Stanley knife gleamed in her hand. She turned and swung the hard steel handle of the Stanley knife heavily into the glass. The glass shook, but didn't shatter or even chip. She hit it again, grunting with the effort, but still it didn't crack.

Stop her, stop her! Robin!

"Don't," Robin said, reaching for her wrist. "You can't."

Scowling in confusion she looked at his hand on her wrist, then at his face. She strained against his grip.

"You can't leave, not until…"

She lashed out, snarling, eyes wild. He tried to fend her off but her fingernails were tearing into his cheeks, scratching toward his eyes.

Screeching in pain Robin threw himself at the floor, twisting and pulling her onto the carpet, trying to pin her under his weight without injuring her.

As quick as a snake, she wriggled out from beneath him and spun, the Stanley knife deadly in her hand.

He barely had time to sit up when she launched at him, slashing at his eyes.

Flinching, he raised his hands and a bright whip of pain slashed across his palms. Blood poured down his wrists.

Obscenely fast, faster than thought, she drew back the blade to strike again.

Robin threw himself backward and managed to bring a foot up to meet her chest. Her vicious slash went wild as she flew backwards and landed on the foyer's red carpet, the Stanley knife clattering out of her hand.

Robin lurched to his feet while she writhed on the floor stunned. His hands wore bloody gloves that dripped freely from his fingers and he leaked from a dozen places.

Not much left, he thought absently. *I'm almost drained.*

He couldn't move quickly enough. Before he had taken two steps towards the knife she rolled into a crouch, sweeping the floor with her hand. When her fingers bumped the blue metal handle she snatched it up, her fixed grimace terrible to behold.

"Wait!" Robin gasped. *"Wait!"*

She leapt at him, a furious demon, the blade swooping at his neck.

All Robin could do was meet her head on, to lean *into* her rather than recoiling... but that was all it took. Deflected, wrong-footed and off-balance, she crashed into him at full speed.

The impact sent them both to the floor again. The knife veered harmlessly off course and slipped from her bloody fingers.

Robin twisted and rolled. She flailed at him, trying to reach his face.

It took all of his strength to fend her hands off, to avoid her vicious nails. She scratched at his arms and cheeks before he managed to seize her slick, bloody wrists. He heard himself snarling.

How can she be so strong?

He managed to push her hands away, lifting her off his body, but with a speed he never would have believed possible she lunged forward and sank her teeth into his neck.

Robin shrieked, a high and shrill scream of agony. Her hard teeth ripped into the soft flesh of his neck and tore it away from his body, head whipping back and forth like a wild animal, shredding flesh and cartilage and tendons.

The world was white. Searing pain. A wet, tearing sound.

The world was agony, then the world was grey, fading towards black.

"Stop." A soft, electric crackle.

He knew that voice. As darkness squeezed everything else away, he *knew* that voice.

"Violet. Stop."

The voice was coming from above.

The tearing at his throat ceased.

He opened his sticky, blurring eyes.

The ceiling was white. The intercom speaker barely visible. Small. Functional. It crackled again. Robin peered at it, trying in vain to lift his head.

Evelyn stood over him, the dripping Stanley knife in her hand.

He tried to move, tried to lift his arms, tried to *anything*. Life poured from his neck, his hands, his side. He could feel every precious drop moving through his veins, every weakening pulse.

One of her rough hands seized a handful of his hair. The other shoved the blade point hard against his throat. He closed his eyes, steeled himself against a last painful thrust. There was a dull rumble, an ominous thrum, a buzzing deep in his mind.

I'm sorry Evelyn.

Time stopped.

I'm dead.

But the blade didn't move. The universe was still. Robin didn't dare breathe, didn't know if a breath was his to take.

She tightened her grip on his hair. When she spoke, her grating voice made him want to weep.

"Let. Me. Out."

The knife pushed more heavily against his throat, but it wouldn't make any difference now.

Dead.

A series of loud, metallic clanks rang out though the foyer.

A familiar sound, a sound Robin would know in his sleep.

The front doors opening.

He felt a tickle of brisk morning air across his bloodied face. The front doors were all wide open, every single door.

The thrumming in his ears was getting louder, the roar of some distant landslide or a rolling thunderstorm, louder and louder by the second. Cool air stroked his cheek. Blood left his body in streams.

This is what dying sounds like. But he could open his eyes. *Not dead yet.*

Evelyn crouched above him, staring at the open doors. The light in her eyes was beatific. She stood, the Stanley knife falling from her slack hand.

The roaring sound made everything shake.

The doors are open.

He tried to sit up, to lunge for the blade, to grab her and stop her... but she was already running for the open doors.

"No... *stop...*"

It was too late. She was outside. She had crossed the threshold.

She had left the cinema.

She didn't look back.

The roar shook the entire building. Tiles vibrated, windows rattled in their frames.

"No!" Laying on the floor, Robin reached for her in vain. The sound was overwhelming, thrumming through his whole body.

Evelyn ran, ran free with her white slip whipping in the wind, her bare feet slapping across the smooth black bitumen of Brisbane Street and as the roaring in Robin's ears reached a crescendo....

A delivery truck smashed into Evelyn's tiny frame. She disappeared beneath the roaring truck's huge, steaming wheels.

Robin tried to cry out but his bubbling throat wouldn't make the sound. With no chance to avoid her the truck hadn't slowed down, but he could hear its airbrakes squealing now as it fishtailed along the empty street. He could see some of what the truck had left in its path.

He turned his head and emptied his stomach on to the floor, gagging. Silver lights danced in front of his eyes.

I'm going to pass out now. But he didn't.

Launceston was slowly waking up – he could hear more trucks rumbling at the TasMilk depot further down Brisbane Street. Soon, the street sweepers would come through.

He vomited again, weak.

I'm still alive. Maybe I'm gonna be okay. He thought about his Uncle David, about his parents on the farm at Karoola. *I should go to hospital.*

Instead, he closed his eyes. Life poured out of him, out of his side, out of his lacerated hands, out of his ruined neck.

He could hear a quiet sobbing.

Evelyn.

The sobbing was resigned, despondent. But it was her. *She's dead, Robin. I'm dead.*

I know. His heart ached. He was exhausted. *I'm so sorry.*
Will you stay with me Robin?
Of course I will. But he was weak. So weak.
We can finish that movie.
Robin smiled - a sad smile, but a smile all the same.
I'd like that.
He died in the muted light of a crisp winter morning.

Epilogue

12 months later

The late shows were packed.

It was a gorgeous evening in Launceston. Stars flickered in the crystalline Tasmanian night while in the soft blue streets below, the frosted windows of bars and cafes glowed orange, promising a warmth embrace and a full belly.

The Majestic Cinema's foyer was bright and lively. There was a carnival atmosphere; *The Matrix*, in its third week, had completely sold out again. Every third punter was wearing thick black sunglasses and every fifth wore a long black trench coat. Some of the more excited geeks were fighting in slow motion down near the men's toilets. No girls in that group.

David smiled as he handed four tickets and a ten dollar note to a young woman on the other side of the ticket box window. He liked seeing the kids in costume. Despite all the shit in the world - or maybe because of it - people still wanted to get lost in a story for a couple of hours. To drift through a dream, to put on a costume and live in a different world for a little while.

The magic of the goddamned movies. He shook his head a little and grinned to himself.

"Next please."

The Candy Bar was busy too. Natalie and Jo dashed about behind the counter, reaching for bags of lollies, flinging pop-corn into buckets and dealing out choc tops with exhilarated smiles. The popcorn machine rattled away and clouds of freshly popped kernels spilled out of its kettle onto the warming tray below. The smell of buttered salt was savoury and welcoming.

There were four paper cups lined up on the soda machine's tray, each filled to the brim. Soda had poured almost constantly from the taps for the last hour. Natalie dropped a fifth cup in the centre of the tray beneath the ice dispenser and cracked the button with her knuckle, then spun away to fetch a bag of Maltesers.

She didn't notice that the cup wasn't quite sitting properly on the tray. She didn't realise that when the ice blocks tumbled into the cup they were likely to send it tumbling over, knocking into the freshly-poured drinks on either side and spilling a litre of soda across the Candy Bar's busy counter...

She didn't notice the empty cup sliding away from the edge, to a steadier position on the tray.

The ice dropped. The cup caught it. *The show goes on.*

David hummed as he closed the ticket box. The cash drawer was full and the punters had been well-behaved. He could count on a quiet night and should be home by midnight.

He closed the Majestic himself now, most nights anyway. He missed Robin, missed him more than he would ever would have expected or admitted, especially on nights like this. While he still couldn't bring himself to clean out the Bunker, or even to unlock it, being at work made him feel closer to his nephew. Another thing he never would have admitted.

Besides, the place was booming. He'd never known the

Majestic to be more profitable than it had been these past few months. The retirement plans he mulled over for so many years – that beach house on Flinders Island – was within reach. But he wasn't ready to go yet. Not just yet.

David's humming turned into a jaunty whistle as he locked the Ticket Box and carried the cash float down to the safe in his office.

Robin watched him go. He liked seeing his uncle so happy.

It would be nice to have a beer with him again. Maybe one day.

He felt the Majestic settle into its usual contented hum. Natalie and Jo were shutting down the Candy Bar – Robin knew they would be done and gone in just a minutes because Natalie was heading to her cousin's twenty-first birthday party straight after work and had spoken of little else all week. The new guy Owen was ducking into the staffroom, presumably to get his jacket and sign off.

None of them noticed the smoke pouring out of Cinemas Two and Three. None of them noticed, because none of them could see it. Robin ignored it as well; the smoke was always there, always billowing, never thinning out or growing more intense, just burning. He stayed away from it.

There were still a few punters left in the foyer. Robin watched a group of three boys lolling on one of the ottomans next to the lightbox posters.

Two of them were looking around furtively. One was holding a large drink cup while the other fumbled a bottle of scotch out of his trench coat pocket. Robin ignored them.

The third kid had a sharpie in his hand and was eyeballing the poster for *Never Been Kissed*. Neither of his friends paid any attention as the kid leaned in, the black sharpie poised to draw a thick line just above Drew Barrymore's earnest, perfectly white smile.

As Robin watched, Drew Barrymore blinked and scowled at the kid's pen.

The kid sat back, eyes wide, the pen waving like a conductor's baton. Drew Barrymore glared at him, furious.

He dropped the pen with a clatter, stood up, and walked away without looking back.

His mates watched him go. They looked at each other. They looked at Drew Barrymore, smiling earnestly into space. One shrugged and they got back to pouring the whisky.

"Having fun?" Robin chuckled.

An arm wrapped around his own. "I am, as a matter of fact." They smiled at each other.

"Well then, another Saturday night." Evelyn wrapped her other arm around him and leaned up for a kiss, which he gave her gladly.

He held her close. "Wanna watch a movie?"

"Yeah." She grinned and kissed him again. "I'd like that."

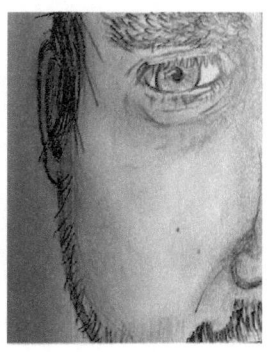

About the Author

Zane Pinner is a writer and digital artist who has worked in children's television, advertising and hospitality. He lives in Tasmania with his gorgeous partner, two boisterous boys and a lazy old brown dog.

You can connect with me on:
- http://studioluckdragon.com
- https://twitter.com/TheTwilightZane
- https://www.facebook.com/zanepinner